Lost Creek Books presents

Wesley Murphey's books—

Fiction

A Homeless Man's Burden: She was only nine

Based on the actual still-unsolved 1960 bean-field murder of little *Alice Lee* near Pleasant Hill and Dexter, Oregon. Wesley Murphey picked in that very field for many years and, as a teen, worked for Alice's father. Murphey's father was Alice's school bus driver and the mail carrier in the area for 25 years. This somewhat autobiographical story begins on the McKenzie River in 2010 with a dying homeless man's confession. (306 pages)

Girl Too Popular

Being the most popular girl in town is not all it's cracked up to be—Carly Cantwell finds out why when she is kidnapped to a remote location in the forest. Is her abductor connected to her ex-stepfather who she rejected? Or is someone or something greater at work here? (176 pages)

To Kill a Mother in Law

Dan Thurmond got more than he bargained for when he married Brenda— a lot more. He got Maureen Muldano, the mother in law from hell. With his marriage on the rocks, and shut out by his wife's restraining order, Dan has taken all he can take. Now his hypocritical, pseudo-spiritual, controlling mother-in-law and the other wolves in her family are going to reap what they sowed. (306 pages)

Trouble at Puma Creek: A Vietnam vet, a deadly hunt

While hunting deer in Oregon's Fall Creek Forest in 1980, Vietnam veteran Roger Bruington is murdered by an Oregon State Police officer after discovering a suspicious shack. Did finding the shack get him killed? Or was this a government hit because Bruington was finally going to reveal the U.S. Government's cover up of the evidence he turned over in 1974 proving American POWs were still being held captive in southeast Asia a year after all POWs were supposedly released? (338 pages)

Nonfiction:

Blacktail Deer Hunting Adventures (172 pages)

A classic. The only true adventure account ever written on hunting the Pacific Coast's blacktail deer. "Anyone who has ever hunted blacktail deer can relate to this book and can gain some good hunting lore from reading it." -- Boyd Iverson author Blacktail Trophy Tactics

Conibear Beaver Trapping in Open Water (110 pages)

Recognized as one of the best beaver trapping books in America.

Coming in 2013:

Fish, Hunt & Trap with the Murpheys (3 volumes approx 172 pges each)
   True Tales and Tactics by Wesley Murphey and his father, Don Murphey
   Includes many articles previously published in national and regional
   publications—and many great never-before-published articles.

Trapping with Wesley Murphey: Beaver, Otter, Raccoon, Nutria and other animals (approx 172 pages)
   Wesley Murphey's many published trapping articles and possibly some
   other stories.

Girl Too Popular

Wesley Murphey

Lost Creek Books
La Pine, Oregon

Girl Too Popular

Published by Lost Creek Books, La Pine, Oregon
http:lostcreekbooks.com

Girl Too Popular is a work of fiction. Names, characters, businesses, places, events and incidents are either the products of the author's imagination or are used in a fictitious manner. Any resemblance to actual persons, living or dead, or actual events is purely coincidental.

Illustrations and Cover Design: Wesley Murphey
Cover Photo: Bridge Creek Falls near Lookout Point Reservoir, OR

ISBN 978-0-9641320-2-3
Library of Congress LCCN 2012900541

Printed in the United States of America by Sheridan Books

Fiction: Teen-Adult Inspirational Suspense

1

The Bridge

The brown-haired, sixteen-year-old girl staggered to the car that her boyfriend had just pulled up to the curb. She knew her parents would ground her if they found out what she had been doing at the party. And they would kill the boy if they knew he was drunk, yet still insisted on driving their daughter home.

Earlier in the evening, the boyfriend's varsity football team at the local high school in Astoria, Oregon had pounded the visiting team from just across the Columbia River in Ilwaco, Washington, 47-6 in its second non-league game of the season. Hopes were high at the high school and in the community that the team could make a run at the state championship this year.

The girl reluctantly got in on the passenger side of the souped-up, blue '68 Chevelle, and said, "I think you're too drunk to drive."

"I'm fine. I can handle my liquor," he slobbered. "You've got nothing to worry about." He revved up the 396 engine causing the car's headers to rumble, then drove the Chevy down several

1

different streets, and finally got to Highway 30, where he turned west.

"You turned the wrong way," she said, obvious concern in her voice.

"I just want to pop over The River for a few minutes and stop by Tommy's house to rub-it-in that we stomped them tonight."

"They're not going to be awake at this hour. And besides, his parents will see you're driving drunk and call the police. That is if we don't get picked up before that."

"Quit being a baby. You always worry too much. I'll have you home in forty-five minutes."

"I don't want to go over The River tonight. Take me home."

"Look, Sue, you're lucky to have me as a boyfriend. You can either go with me now, or we're through and I'll date one of the school hotties instead."

She considered herself very lucky to be dating the star quarterback on the football team, so she said, "Okay, I'll go along this time, but never again. You could get someone killed driving drunk."

"I'm not drunk; just a little tipsy. Believe me I can still drive just fine."

Two minutes later, as they were nearing the peak on the southern end of the Astoria-Megler Bridge, 200 feet above the Columbia River below, the Chevelle quickly approached a brown 1985 Ford pickup going the same direction.

"The guy driving that pickup is obviously a drunk, to be driving that slowly," he said. "Watch this: I'm going to give him a scare."

"Please don't, Bryan!"

He stomped down on the accelerator and ran right up on the back of the pickup, made a quick weave into the left lane to pass, then cranked the steering wheel back hard to the right to cut the guy off. But he cut too soon and his rear end clipped the left front fender of the pickup.

"No!" Sue screamed, as the Chevelle immediately rolled over to the left.

Sue, not wearing a seatbelt, was ejected out the passenger-side window in front of the Chevelle, which rolled over her. Bryan, who wasn't buckled in either, tried to hang on to the steering wheel, but the force of the roll was too powerful. He was thrown around inside the car like a crash dummy, but somehow wasn't ejected.

On impact, the Ford pickup veered hard to the right and hit the concrete siding. The driver tried to control it, but the truck careened off the concrete and came back across the highway toward the rolling Chevelle, then plowed into the left side of the bridge, seventy feet from where the crash began.

Bryan felt as if every bone in his body was broken, yet he was still conscious. He grabbed the steering wheel of his car that had landed right-side up and pulled himself up to look out the window. Just then, the male voice on his car stereo, sang, "Oh where, oh where can my baby be…"

He cried out in pain and searched the highway for Sue. He spotted her body laying in the middle of the road sixty feet away, in the direction they had come from. He felt blood run down his face and then found the gash in his head with his bloody fingers.

As he stared helplessly at Sue's motionless body, suddenly, the Ford pickup, just to the right of his line of sight, burst into flames.

Bryan tried to push open the driver's door of his car, but it wouldn't budge. He lunged for the passenger's door, but found it jammed too. He crawled through the broken passenger window, just in time to see the man, his clothes on fire, come around from the back of the burning pickup and run to the edge of the bridge. He knew what the man was going to do. He tried to yell, "No. It's too far down to the water." But no words came.

Then the burning man, moaning from pain, climbed over the side of the bridge and leapt out into the darkness. Bryan was too badly injured to get to the edge of the road to look over. He slowly crawled along the pavement, trying to get to Sue. Then he passed out.

2

All-star

11 years later—

"She made first team all-league in basketball last year, as a sophomore," said Kaylin, an attractive dark-haired, nicely built junior at Roseburg High School.

"She's everyone's pet," said Melissa. "I can't stand her."

"Yeah, I know what you mean," chimed in Heather. "All the boys whistle when she walks by."

"Or belch," said another.

"It must be nice to be the best at everything you do."

"You guys are just jealous," said Kristin, a fellow basketball player.

"Oh, so why are you sticking up for her?"

"If you spent much time around her, you'd know she isn't that hung up on herself."

"Where have you been?"

"She and I used to be best friends," said Kristin.

5

"So why doesn't she hang around with you now?"

"You know how it goes sometimes when a girl gets a boyfriend. They don't have much time for you anymore."

"Doesn't that tell you something?"

"Like what?"

"That she was just using you before."

"I don't believe that."

"Then you're pretty naïve."

"What a coincidence. Here come the king and queen now."

Carly and Jeff walked past, arm in arm, as the seven girls huddled around Kaylin's locker.

"See, she didn't even notice us."

"The Ho."

"You guys can be so obnoxious," said Kristin.

"We're teens, what do you expect?"

"I wouldn't want to get on your bad sides. I can imagine what you'd say about me."

"You should hear what we say about you already."

"Funny."

Just then, Melissa's phone rattled. She read the text message from her friend at the far end of the hall. "Stud alert. Three headed your way now."

In a second, three of the varsity wrestlers, wearing their muscle tank tops on their way to the locker room to get dressed for practice, came into view.

"That Sam is one hunk of a man," said Kristin, describing the boy in the middle. "He took sixth in state last year at 171."

"Yeah, and he just broke up with Marie."

"He's mine."

"Only in your dreams."

"I'll take Kyle, the one on the left."

"He's already spoken for."

"Not when I make *my move*."

"What are you going to use, 'a cradle'?" They all laughed.

The approaching wrestlers noticed the girls and figured they were being talked about. They winked, smiled and tightened up their muscles as they walked past. That time in the weight room paid more dividends than just on the mat.

That evening—

The crowd of three hundred fifty stood and cheered loudly, as Carly Cantwell drove the ball down the center of the key, drawing defensive attention from the right side. She quickly dished off to Camille Olson on the right baseline, who broke for the basket and laid it in.

Newberg 51 Roseburg 50, with forty seconds to go.

After two weeks of early-season non-league action, the state-wide poll had Newberg ranked number two and Roseburg number six. But many people believed tonight's game could be a preview of the state-championship game that would take place in three months.

"Defense. Defense," the crowd yelled, stomping feet on the wooden bleachers.

"Man! Man!" yelled Roseburg coach Flash Hollister, as his girls hustled back down the court, sticking close to their opponents.

The clock slowly ticked off as the Newberg point guard crossed the half-court line, hounded by Carly.

"Weave!" yelled her coach.

The Newberg girls spread the floor with a girl in each corner. The two girls at the corner of the baselines each broke up court to set picks for the wings. As the left wing broke past her defender toward the key, coach Hollister and the girls on the bench next to him yelled, "Switch!"

But Kristin's legs got tangled, and she fell to the floor. The Newberg girl had a clear path to the basket, as she took the bounce pass from the point guard and laid the ball in the hole, just before Camille could reach her.

Newberg 53 Roseburg 50, nineteen seconds left and counting.

Carly took the inbounds pass and quickly sprinted up the floor, but was met just beyond mid-court with a trap. She juked to her left and passed the ball to Kristin on the right. Then she sprinted toward the right side of the key where the center and Camille had set a pick wall. Kristin hit her with a hard overhand pass. She stopped suddenly behind the wall and put up a fourteen-foot jumper. Swish. 53-52.

"Man Press!" yelled Hollister.

As Newberg got the ball in and dribbled up the left side of the backcourt, the crowd yelled, "Ten. Nine. Eight.

"Trap! Trap!"

Two Roseburg girls trapped the Newberg ball handler and one of them swatted the ball into the center of the court. Carly picked it up and sprinted to the basket, dribbling the ball with her right hand. With a step on her defender, she laid the ball in, just as the crowd counted, "Four...Three."

"Timeout!" yelled the entire Newberg team.

The referees' whistles blew. Two point four seconds on the clock.

Roseburg 54 Newberg 53.

When the time-out was over, a Newberg girl set up out-of-bounds under the basket, while her four team-mates lined up single file just outside the key on the right side in the backcourt. Roseburg defended with two girls on the baseline and three spread at the half-court line.

The referee handed the ball to the Newberg girl, she slapped the ball immediately, and her team mates spread out. Two broke up the floor to just short of the half-court line and one headed to the right side of the front court. They were picked up at once by the three Roseburg defenders. The girl out of bounds sprinted hard to her left and managed to get the ball to her team-mate who broke part-way up the floor on the same side.

The team-mate immediately passed the ball up court to a gal breaking across half-court.

"One," yelled the raucous crowd.

It was too late. The Roseburg girls trapped the Newberg girl; she couldn't even throw up a long prayer of a shot.

"Roseburg! Roseburg! Roseburg!" the crowd shouted in unison.

3

Taken

Six weeks later, Tuesday evening, February 2nd—

The Roseburg girls had beaten league rival North Medford at home 59-54 half an hour ago, bringing their league record to 8 wins against 1 loss, and their overall record to 15-1, ranked fourth in the state. Their only loss of the season was a four-point shocker on the road to little-regarded South Eugene.

As the last of the girls were leaving the dressing room, Carly Cantwell said goodbye to the remaining two girls. Then she walked across the lighted parking lot on the clear, brisk night, carrying her duffle bag and back pack.

Most nights following practice, her boyfriend, Jeff Lydle—a six-foot three-inch, two-hundred-pound, senior starting forward on the varsity boys basketball team—would be with her and would give her a ride home in his 1995 Pontiac. But on game nights, like tonight, the girls and boys often played at opposite high schools. Tonight his team was on the road at North Medford and wouldn't arrive back to Roseburg High School for nearly three more hours,

10

allowing time for the team to stop at McDonald's in Grants Pass after the game. He had text messaged her just a few minutes before she left the locker room saying his team had just won the game 71-70 in overtime, to remain in a tie for second in the league, a game out of first.

When Carly reached the vehicle that her older brother had let her use, a blue 2006 Ford Explorer that was parked farther away from the gym than she liked, she pushed the button on the remote key and heard the car door locks release. As she started to lift the door handle to open the driver's door, suddenly, she was grabbed around the waist by an obviously big and strong man. At the same time he pulled her head back and placed a rag over her mouth and nose. As she started to struggle, she smelled something funny, then passed out.

The man slung her five-foot seven-inch, one hundred forty pound limp body over his right shoulder, and jogged away from the parking lot, leaving her two bags lying on the pavement next to the explorer. He cut through a field that contained numerous old apple trees and long, brown grass that had been beaten down by frost and rain.

In five minutes, he reached the old dirt road where his brown 1985 Ford pickup was parked, opened the passenger door, laid Carly on the seat, then placed a black straight jacket on her over her black Roseburg High sports jacket and fastened it, securing her arms across her stomach. He then duct-taped her ankles together and bent her legs before closing the door and going around to his side and getting in. After he got in and started the truck's engine, he drove the truck to the main highway, half a mile away.

Just after they hit the pavement and headed up the highway, the man placed an ammonia capsule under Carly's nose to awaken her. She coughed a couple times. Then he placed a strip of duct tape over her mouth, just as she came to.

She tried to scream, but couldn't get the sound past the tape. She kicked her feet out and hit the heating duct in the right corner of the cab.

"Settle down," the man said. "You're alright."

She turned her head, the top of which was up against the man's right hip, as much as she could to look at him. He was wearing a long, black trench coat, with gloves on his hands and a rubber Halloween mask of an old man over his whole head. She tried to scream again and to move her body away from him, but it was futile.

"You need to relax. We're going for a long ride."

She couldn't believe this was happening to her. She longed for Jeff, or her older brothers, to be here, to rescue her. She didn't know how long she had been unconscious, but felt it couldn't have been too long. She thought of her mom, older brothers and sister who would be at Marie Callendar's right now, waiting for her before ordering their desserts. She wanted so bad to be with them. This couldn't be happening to her. But it was. What did he want? What was he going to do to her? Please, God, don't let him hurt me, or kill me. She cried silently, soaking the seat under her head with her tears.

At Marie Callendar's, Carly's mom, Glenda Reeves, was growing more and more impatient by the minute. It was now nearly an hour after the game had ended. Carly should have arrived fifteen or twenty minutes ago.

"Mom, she isn't answering her cell phone," said Marsha, Carly's twenty-nine-year-old sister.

"She doesn't give two hoots about us and our time," said Carly's mom. "She's so wrapped up in herself and all the attention she always gets that she thinks no one else exists—at least no one outside her circle of friends, her boyfriend and her sports."

"Don't you think you're being a little hard on her, Mom," said thirty-one-year-old Darren, Carly's oldest brother.

"She's a good kid; she just gets sidetracked," said Marsha. "We all used to do the same thing."

"Not like her, you didn't," said Carly's mom. "She's definitely the untamed one in the family. It's a good thing Grandma wasn't feeling well enough tonight for her and Grandpa to come out for pie after the game. She would have had a cow by now."

"Yeah, you're right about that. Grandma embarrasses Grandpa all the time," said Bill, the youngest brother at twenty-eight.

"Not just Grandpa."

"You know her, she says what she thinks, and *it doesn't matter who is listening or who it will hurt.*"

"I think she's harder on Carly than anyone," said Marsha. "Yet, she brags about her sports, her academic accomplishments, her music and anything and everything else she does, to anyone who will listen."

"Not to just anyone who will listen, sis," Bill corrected, "just plain old anyone, whether they want to hear it or not."

"Listening to Grandma talking about Carly in a crowd, you'd think no one else had grand-kids," said Darren. "I bet people get sick of listening to her brag about her granddaughter. Did she brag about the rest of us like that, Mom?"

"Not that much. Of course none of you were as successful in so many things like she is. But she's always bragged about her kids and grandkids more than anyone I know."

"Well, with Carly there's a lot to brag about," said Marsha. "First or second team all-league in everything she does. First trumpet in the band, Homecoming Queen, selected to go to Washingon, D.C. on the debate team. You name it."

Fifteen minutes later—

"Mom, something isn't right," said Marsha. "She's still not answering her cell phone even though we've left three messages, the last two saying we're worried."

"I think we better drive over to the high school and see, if by chance, she's still there or something," said Darren.

Ten minutes later, in the Roseburg High School parking lot, talking on cell phones—

"Mom, my explorer is still here," said Darren, his wife and two daughters in the car with him—Bill and his girlfriend following right behind them.

"Maybe she went with a friend," said Mom, trying to ease her own concern. "I know Jeff's team was playing away tonight, so it wouldn't have been him."

As Darren got closer, "Mom, her bags are laying on the pavement next to the vehicle. Something's definitely wrong."

"No! Don't tell me that, son. Marsha and I will be right there."

Eight minutes later, the Roseburg police were on the site and questioning the family. Carly's mom had already called Coach Hollister and some of Carly's team-mates and friends, a couple of which had already arrived in the parking lot. But no one knew anything about where she might be. Her cell phone was found in her duffle bag. The police were pretty sure it was a kidnapping.

4

The Falls

After more than two hours on the road, the man pulled the pickup down a rough gravel road. The bouncing around upset Carly's bladder, and she tried to sit up. The man held her down and said, "I'll get you out so you can go in a few minutes."

She groaned. She wanted so bad to be able to talk... to ask why he took her... to plead for her safety. She cried some more. God, don't let him hurt me.

Twenty minutes later, he stopped the truck and turned off the engine. He helped her sit up. She looked beside the truck, but could only see slight shadows. She knew they were deep in the woods. She looked up through the windshield and saw the tops of what looked like fir or cedar trees barely visible against the moonless night sky. Where has he taken me? Why me?

He got out and came around the back of the truck, opened her door, and removed the duct tape from her ankles. She was scared to death.

Suddenly it dawned on her that she could hear water, like falls.

She tried to think of where there would be waterfalls, then realized these falls could be anywhere within three hours of Roseburg. They could be a hundred fifty miles away from her home... or more. God, help me, please.

She hadn't given God much thought in the last couple years, even though her mom still made her go to church most Sundays. Who was her mom to make her go to church anyway? She argued with her mom about that every week. "I'm old enough to decide for myself whether I want to go to church."

"As long as you live in my house, young lady," her mom always said, "you *will* attend church."

What good did church ever do her? She'd already been divorced four times and was single again. What kind of an example was she? What right did she have to make me do anything?

The man pulled her out of the truck. She tried to scream—but again, pointless.

"I'll remove the tape from your mouth now, but it won't do you any good to scream here. There's no one around for miles. If you scream enough, you might even draw in a bear, a cougar or some coyotes that think they might be able to get an easy meal. I don't think you want that, do you?"

She shook her head, no.

He removed the tape, then wiped the tears from her cheeks.

"Don't cry, Carly. Please don't cry."

"How do you know my name?"

"Don't ask any questions right now. As long as you cooperate, you'll be okay."

"What are you going to do to me? Why did you take *me*?"

"No questions now."

With him standing directly in front of her, she thought about kneeing him in the groin and making a break for it. Right, with a straight jacket on? I'd only make him mad at me. Later. God, please let there be a later.

He led her in between a couple of alder trees off to the right.

"No!" she screamed. "Please don't—"

"Take it easy. I said I'd let you go to the bathroom, and that's what I'm going to do."

The roar of the falling water was loud now. She sensed they were standing near the edge of a cliff. Then she saw the white spray of the stream down below her. The waterfall was to the left.

Any other time she would have thought the falls sounded wonderful. She loved waterfalls. But tonight the rumble of the water only made her heart ache more. She felt so lonely. She was so scared. Who was this animal that would take a young woman—*her*—away from everything she knew to such a lonely place, deep in the woods?

"I'm going to unfasten your arms now, so you can do what you need to do. I'll be right behind these trees. Don't do anything stupid." He freed her arms, then walked twenty feet away, and faced in the opposite direction.

When she came back out, he refastened her arms and helped her get back in the truck. He then put a cloth around her head to cover her eyes, and said, "We've got to drive a little farther, so relax."

"Why can't you leave my eyes uncovered and my arms free?"

"I have my reasons. Like I said, now is not the time for questions."

5

The Hike

As they drove down the road, the man said, "You played a great game tonight, 21 points. Your season high, wasn't it?"

"You were at the game? You sat through my game waiting to kidnap me? What kind of man are you anyway?"

"This isn't about me. But you'll figure that out soon enough. Don't ask me anymore questions now."

Twenty minutes later, the man parked the truck and got out. It was now 1:30 a.m., Wednesday morning.

"We've got to walk from here," he said.

"Where are we going?" Carly asked. "Please, mister. I just want to go home. I don't deserve this."

"You think these things happen because someone deserves them to?"

"I don't know," she cried. "I just know I want to live. I don't want you to hurt me. Please, just take me back to the school."

"I can't do that. That's not your destiny. Not now."

My destiny. This guy's crazy. I'm with a crazy man. Please God, don't let my destiny end out here. I don't deserve this.

"I'll tell you this—and I don't want to have to tell you again—it will go best for you if you do exactly as I say and don't talk to me until I tell you to. You're no match for me physically, so there's no point in getting aggressive. We have a short, rugged hike ahead of us. I know you're in good shape, so it shouldn't be any problem for you. Do you understand?"

"Yes."

As he unfastened her arms and took the straight jacket off, she sized him up. She figured him to be about six-foot-two and well over two hundred pounds. He was right: she was no match for him. She wanted to see him without the mask, but doubted she'd ever get the chance.

But if he is planning to kill me, he doesn't need to keep the mask on, right? If I'm dead, I'll never be able to identify him anyway. Maybe he isn't planning to kill me. Or maybe he is and he's just keeping the mask on so that I can't scratch his face. Oh God, don't let him kill me.

He tied a rope around her waist and gave her a mag-lite, then grabbed the free end of the rope and gave a tug. "Let's go." He shined his flashlight ahead and walked into the thick salal bushes.

After following him for several minutes, she thought she heard the slight sound of water. Then she knew she did. They must be approaching a stream. The farther they hiked, the louder the water sounded, until it was a roar; must be a waterfall. She suddenly felt very thirsty. She wanted to ask the man where he was taking her.

She tried to figure out what direction they were headed by looking for the moon. She knew the moon always crossed the sky to the south, from east to west. But there was no moon now. And the trees overhead prevented her from seeing the big dipper.

She thought back to the song she learned in first grade, "Mr. Moon, Mr. Moon, you're out too soon, the sun is still in the sky. Go back to your bed, and cover up your head, and wait 'til the day goes by." This must have been one of those days when the moon came out too soon. She longed to be that little first grade girl right now, safe in her classroom, singing silly songs.

Maybe this man has a soft side. Maybe I should start singing. Music can touch people like nothing else, maybe even a crazy man like him.

But she kept silent.

Finally, in the light of her mag-lite, she saw a twelve-foot-wide flowing stream just ahead. The roar of the waterfall was off to their right. They were just above the falls. The man led her to the right for about thirty feet and then she saw the waterfall.

The man said, "Okay, we have to climb down this cable ladder."

He pulled it from the bushes and unfurled it down the face of the rocky cliff they were standing on. She noticed it was secured to two alder trees, several feet back from the cliff.

…A cable ladder way out here in the woods? He had this whole thing planned ahead of time. Why me?

"You've done very well not speaking, up until now," said the man. "That goes in your favor. If you continue to do what I ask, I will be pleased."

'He will be pleased?' What's that mean, that he might not kill me?

"I'm going to go first, to stabilize the cable. You follow me as soon as I'm far enough down to allow you room to get your feet on. If you try to run away while I'm on the ladder, it won't do you any good. You don't have any idea where we are. I know these woods like the back of my hand, even in the dark. And there are a lot of wild animals out here, including bears and cougars. Do you understand?"

"Yes."

After climbing down perhaps fifteen feet, she could feel the mist of cold water, sprayed from the falls, on the back of her head and on her hands. It got wetter the farther down they climbed. Finally, they reached a rocky shelf. She didn't know how far down they had climbed.

She looked up and saw stars, but could barely make out the top of the cliff. She couldn't get any feel for distance, but estimated it had to be at least thirty or forty feet. She shined her light around to scope things out. They were surrounded on three sides by nothing but sheer rocky cliffs, partially covered by damp moss and a smattering of ferns. The final side was a deep drop-off where the stream fell farther into the canyon. Do we have to climb down that too, she wondered.

"Go ahead and get a drink from the creek," he said. "You're probably pretty thirsty by now."

"Is it safe to drink?"

"I wouldn't tell you to get a drink if it wasn't. This is pure mountain water. 'It doesn't get any better than this.'"

Like, right. He's planning to kill me. What does he care about whether I could catch some disease from this water?

"See. I'll drink from it myself." He squatted down and dipped his cupped hands into the thirty-foot-long pool, then sipped the refreshing water from them. He repeated that several times, then said, "Your turn."

Carly followed his example, squatted and drank from the stream. Any other time she would have thought and said, "This is to die for." But not tonight.

After she finished drinking and stood back up, he said, "Follow me."

He walked twenty feet to the left edge of the waterfall, then pushed aside a long, thick, damp strand of spaghetti-like moss that was hanging from a slight ledge about twelve feet above him. Behind the moss there was an opening. He stepped in. She followed. It was a cavern. She was terrified. This is where he's going to do it. God, help me, she prayed.

They walked in about ten feet, then she saw it. Ahead of them in the huge rocky cave was what looked like the front of a shack. She saw numerous rough-sawn, six-inch-wide boards mounted vertically.

Since he hadn't told her to be quiet when she asked about the water, she chanced, "What is this place?"

"It's my home."

"You live clear out here in no man's land, deep in the mountains, all by yourself? What kind of a guy would want to do that?" Immediately, she wished she hadn't said that last part.

"This is just one of my homes. What kind of guy do you think I am, anyway?"

She didn't know what to say, whether to say what she really thought, or to make up something that might not offend him or set him off. She didn't say anything.

After too long, "Well, answer my question."

"I don't know," she took the safe route.

He didn't follow it up. Instead he turned toward the planks and opened a hidden door.

"Come on, let's go in," he said.

She was trembling. She could only imagine what he planned to do to her in there.

After he walked through the door, she sneaked a quick look at her watch. It was 2:20. Up until now, she had been so high on fear adrenaline that she hadn't felt anything *but fear*. But suddenly she felt exhausted. She wanted to sleep. She wanted to be home in her bed, asleep. Would she ever get to sleep in her own bed again? God, let me sleep in my own bed again. She cried silently. Her knees buckled. She fell to the ground, unconscious.

6

Prime Suspect

By the next morning, Wednesday, practically everyone in Roseburg knew that Carly Cantwell, the star of the Roseburg High girls' basketball team, was missing. The local radio and television stations were broadcasting the news every half hour:

Carly Faye Cantwell, a sixteen-year-old junior, was reported missing last night at 10:10, an hour after leaving the Roseburg High School girls' locker room, following her varsity basketball game. Her backpack and duffle bag were found laying next to her brother's blue 2006 Ford Explorer, Oregon license plate OSM249 that was parked in the southeast corner of the south gymnasium parking lot. She was supposed to have driven the explorer to Marie Callendars to meet with her family after the game.

Cantwell is five-feet seven inches, weighs approximately 140 pounds, has long, blond hair, and was last seen wearing blue jeans, a pink long-sleeve shirt, her black Roseburg High jacket and high top tennis shoes. **If anyone witnessed anyone doing anything suspicious near the described vehicle at any time last night, or saw any suspicious vehicles in the area surrounding the high school and outlying area, or if anyone has seen or heard from Ms. Cantwell, please contact the Douglas County Sheriff, Oregon State Police, or the Roseburg Police.**

At the sheriff station, Wednesday morning, further questioning—

"Ms. Reeves, is it possible that Carly could have staged this thing for any reason?" asked Lieutenant Bond Hampton, criminal investigator for the Douglas County Sheriff Department.

"How can you imply such a thing at a time like this?" answered Ms. Reeves, Carly's mom.

"I don't mean to offend you with that question, but stranger things have happened, especially with teenagers."

"Well my daughter would never pull something like that. She was kidnapped."

"Many times kids *are* taken by a stranger," said Hampton. "But sometimes the perpetrator is someone they know, such as a non-custodial parent. Does Carly have a father, or can you think of anyone who might have known your daughter that could have taken her?"

Carly's mom cried. Then, getting a bit of a grip, said, "Now that you mention it, my ex-husband, her ex-stepfather, is capable of something like this. Yes. He's very capable of something like this, just to get back at me, and because he never did like Carly, or all the attention she received."

"So you think he might have taken her?" he asked.

"It's definitely possible."

"What's his name, ma'am, and where does he live?"

"His name is Kenneth Dean Roderick. He lives in Chemult."

"How long were you married to him and when did you break

up?"

"We got married in 1999, and I left him two years ago. The divorce was final ten months ago."

"Was he ever violent toward you or Carly?"

"Not physically, but he abused us psychologically."

Hampton thought, great, another one of these.

He questioned her further, then contacted the Klamath County Sheriff's Department to get one of its officers to check out the lead on Ken Roderick, Carly's ex-stepfather.

On Wednesday evening, the Klamath County Sheriff's deputy reported back to Hampton that, so far, they had been unable to locate Roderick. He wasn't at his home, and no one seemed to know where he was or when he might be back. Neither did anyone know where his two adult kids or his siblings lived to try to contact them. From what law enforcement could determine, he was a private man.

Carly woke up, soaked in sweat and trembling. She'd had a terrible nightmare. The worst she'd ever had, or could ever imagine. It was still dark. It couldn't be time to get up for school yet, could it? The alarm couldn't have gone off already. She still felt tired. Last night's game had taken a lot out of her, but it was great. **It's what she lived for**: sports, tight games, huge crowds, game-winning shots, *the attention.*

Then she noticed the muffled sound of water off to her right. She wiped the sleep from her eyes and looked around the room. *This isn't my room.*

Then she remembered.

"No!" she screamed. "God, no! Please let this be a dream."

But it wasn't a dream. She wasn't home. She was hours from home, from her room, from her mom, from her brothers and sister. From her friends, from Jeff. God, don't let this be real. But it was real.

Where am I? Where is *he*?

As she focused, she noticed a shaft in the rocky ceiling above her that let in a little light from somewhere. The shaft was very long, but there was light at the end. She sensed a slight draft. It was fresh air. It must open to the outside.

She looked around her in the dim light. She was inside a small room, maybe twelve feet by twelve feet. The room had wooden walls on two sides, while the other two sides were rock walls, the sides of the cave. Foot-wide wooden planks were the floor. In one corner was a small dresser; a small table and chair were in another. There was an old-fashioned oil lamp on the table. Off to one side of the table was a propane tank and heater.

In other circumstances, she would have been fascinated with this cavern beneath the waterfalls. But now all she could think about was that she had to escape, and soon, before the man got back to do what he planned to do to her.

Just then, a door swung open to the outside. The big man with the old-man mask came in. She shook violently. He would do her now. She screamed.

"It's okay. Don't be afraid," he said, then immediately lit the oil lamp on the table.

She cried. "I want to go home. Please, mister, let me go home."

"I can't do that."

"Why can't you do that?"

"Why would I take you, just to turn around and let you go?"

"Why would you take me at all? I'm a good kid. I don't deserve this. I'm popular. Everyone likes me. People will miss me. They'll send the cops to get you."

"There you go again, saying you don't deserve this. Do you think that everything that happens to people is about what they deserve?"

"Bad things happen to bad people because they deserve them to," she said. "Not to good kids like me."

"You really have things figured out, don't you?" he said rhetorically. "Believe it or not, life isn't all about you. I know that's probably hard for you to believe, since you seem to be the center of attention in everything you do."

"How would you know that?" she asked. "What do you know about me? Who are you? Why are you doing this to me?"

"Why *not* to you?"

"What do you want from me? I don't deserve this."

"It's always all about you, isn't it? You think the whole world revolves around you. You're just a tiny thing in this world. Yet, in *your* mind, you are *IT*."

"You're a cruel man."

She couldn't believe she just said that. She was going to get herself killed. Why couldn't she keep her mouth shut? Sometimes she reminded herself of Grandma, and Mom, and Aunt Maggie.

None of them could ever seem to keep their mouths shut—especially Grandma.

"You don't know anything about me," he said.

"You took an innocent teen girl from everything important to her. You plan to hurt me. To kill me. To—"

"You know nothing, Carly! You have much to learn, and very little time to learn it in."

Little time. He *is* going to kill me. He's going to kill me *soon.* But why do I have much to learn if he's going to kill me? Why learn anything if I'm going to be dead anyway?

"I have to go now," he said, "but I'll be back soon. When you have to go to the bathroom, there's a little toilet room back through that false wall there." He pointed to the wall near the foot of the cot she was on. "It's like the old outhouses, but much better. There's no light in there, so you'll have to take either the oil lamp or the maglite. Do you know how to work an oil lamp?"

"Yes, my grandpa showed me."

"Don't think about trying to escape. There's no way out of here."

"What time is it?"

"Time doesn't matter here."

"But you said I have little time. What's that mean?"

"You'll find out."

He turned and left.

As he walked out of the room, she noticed the gold letters on the back of the purple windbreaker he was now wearing said, "*Astoria Fishermen Booster Club.*"

7

Alone

After he left, Carly laid back the sleeping bag from on top of her, grabbed the mag-lite off the table and looked at her watch. She was shocked to see it was 3:30 in the afternoon. She couldn't believe she had slept that long. She cautiously opened the false door at the end of the bed, afraid of what she might find back there. Shining her flashlight in, she observed that the room was quite small, maybe five feet across. She heard a trickle of water to her left and shined the light there. There was a rock bench a foot and a half above the rock floor, with a wooden toilet seat on it, over what looked like a natural rock bowl about a foot across. The trickle she had heard was a stream of water about three inches wide that ran down the sloped cave wall and into the make-shift toilet. She knew it must wash the waste away.

When she was done in the little room, she went back into the main room and tried to think of an escape plan. The man said he'd be back soon. Should she try to get away now, or hope for a chance later, maybe when he left for a longer time? But if she didn't escape now, would she even be alive later? She had to go now. Fifteen minutes had passed since he left without saying where he was going.

Then she noticed a loaf of French bread, a pitcher of water, and a glass on the table. She hadn't seen them before. He must have put them there right after she went into the toilet room. She wondered if the bread might be poisoned. Her stomach was growling. She didn't even get to eat the blackberry pie that she had planned to order at Marie Callendars last night. She took a chance that the bread was safe and wolfed into it. She ate nearly half the loaf, and drank half the pitcher of water along with it.

When she had eaten her fill, she re-tied her shoe laces. Then she pushed the outer door open and looked out. The waterfall roared, but she couldn't see it because of the long strands of spaghetti-like moss hanging from the cave roof.

She stepped ahead, then pushed the moss to one side and peered out. Daylight. The waterfalls. Fresh air. It was beautiful. It was warm, she guessed in the mid-fifties. She walked out to the edge of the long, deep pool below the falls. What if he had just gone a short distance, or even worse, was out there hiding—waiting to see if she tried to escape? Then when he caught her he would hurt her for sure.

In the canyon, the fir and cedar trees on the side of the mountain completely shaded the stream. It would be dark in a little over two hours. She oriented herself by the shadows. She knew the sun set in the west, so since the shade came from her left, that meant that the stream flowed to the north. If only she had an idea where she was, which stream this was.

She knew the man had driven her a long ways—at least three hours—from Roseburg. The Cascade Mountains to the east of Roseburg were loaded with snow this time of year. But there was no snow here. She couldn't be in the Cascade Mountains. He must have driven somewhere toward the Pacific Ocean to the west then, somewhere in the Oregon Coastal Mountains.

What streams in the coastal mountains flowed north? She didn't have a clue. It didn't matter anyway; a stream could turn a different direction in just a short distance. She had to be in the headwaters of some stream. That's where most waterfalls were found: where the country was steep. Her stepfather had taught her that. In fact, he had taught her a lot about surviving in the wild and how you could tell directions. Things like the sun will always be directly south at twelve noon, unless it was daylight savings time; then it was due south at one pm. The "Sunsetswest" in the Pacific Ocean. Moss grows thickest on the north side of trees, where there is less light and more moisture. That the moon moves across the sky from east to west and many more things.

But if this was the Coast Range Mountains, she thought, then Roseburg and home were to the east. Once she got out of the canyon, she would go east. *If she* got out of the canyon.

She realized that the cable ladder they had come down last night was nowhere around. She looked up the cliff on her right, where she figured they had descended from. It was at least thirty-five feet to the top of the cliff there. There was no sign of the cable. As she looked around her, all she saw was cliff face, shale rock, moss and some small ferns growing out of the rock. She was suddenly filled with despair. She cried.

There had to be a way. What about down the falls below her?

She walked over to the right edge of the rock ledge and leaned out as far as she could without going over. This next fall had to be even farther down than the one by the cavern was up. And there was no way to climb down. Besides what good would it do? Just take her deeper into the canyon. She needed to get up and out of the canyon. Please, God, help me.

She knew she could never figure out a way to get out of here before dark, so she resigned herself to being at the man's mercy for another night. After drinking some stream water, she went back inside.

8

Other Girls?

Suddenly, she thought, if he took me, then maybe he's taken some other girls in the past. What if he did take them and killed them in here. There might be blood. Not if he just strangled them. She lit the oil lamp and held it. She got down on her hands and knees and went around the entire room looking closely for any signs of blood. There, under the edge of the cot, near a leg. A spot about an inch around. Yes, it was dried blood. Maybe not. Could it be ketchup or something else that just looks like blood? She bent close to smell it, but there was no odor. God, don't let it be blood.

She heard something outside. The door creaked open. It was him.

"What are you doing down there, Carly?"

"I... uh... I thought I heard something run under the cot... something like a mouse or something."

"Did you see anything?"

"Uh... no."

"I do find mice in here occasionally," said the man. "But they don't last long."

"Why don't they last long?"

"They die."

What did he mean? Like how do they die? She didn't dare ask. She got up and put the lamp back on the table.

"There are some extra clothes for you in the dresser there," he motioned to the corner.

"Your clothes won't fit me."

"They're not my clothes."

"Whose clothes are they then?" she stammered. Why do you have anyone else's clothes here in this cave, she wondered; did you kill the girl, or girls, who wore them?

"It doesn't matter. They'll fit you. Now take a seat on the cot. I want to talk to you." He sat down on the lone chair next to the wooden table.

"Tell me about your father."

"I don't have a father," she answered, while thinking, this man *is* crazy. The first thing he wants me to talk about is a father?

"You have to have a father. You wouldn't be here without one."

Something about his voice sounded vaguely familiar. She had thought so earlier, but now she was sure. She dredged her mind, but couldn't place it.

"My mom never lived with my birth father. It was just a short physical relationship. That's what she said."

"What happened to him?"

"She met him at a bar one lonely night. They dated for a few months. He was a drug addict and alcoholic. She finally told him to get lost."

"But he was still your father, right?"

"Sort of. I rarely saw him. Then he ended up getting locked in prison for some terrible crimes. After being there for six months, a prison gang killed him. I was five when that happened."

"I'm sorry about that."

"Don't be. He was nothing to me."

"That's awfully cold of you, don't you think—to say that about the man that caused you to be born?"

"He was a worthless piece of humanity. I don't want to talk about him anymore."

"So you never had any other fathers?" No step-fathers?"

"Can we not talk about that now?"

"You have nothing else to do now than to talk to me. And *you are* going to talk to me, like it or not. I know you aren't used to *not* having things your own way, but up here you'll do what I tell you to do, and talk when I tell you to. Up here the world doesn't revolve around you."

She knew he was right. If she didn't talk to him, she knew he would probably kill her like he must have done to the other girls whose clothes were in the dresser, and whose blood was still on the floor.

She started crying. "I want to go home."

"I know that. Kids always want to go home."

What is he saying? How many kids has he had up here? She wanted to ask about the other kids, but was afraid of the answer.

"Getting back to the father thing," he said. "So have you had any step-fathers?"

"Yes. One"

"When?"

"My mom married him when I was six and ditched him for good two years ago, when I was almost fifteen."

"How many husbands has your mom had?"

"Four; and I guess she shacked up with one or two others. Not the greatest example. Why are you asking me about my fathers?"

"I just want to hear what you have to say about them."

"There's nothing to say."

"Your mom's last husband was your stepfather for eight years and there's nothing to say?"

"That's right."

"What kind of guy was he?"

"Just your average jerk stepfather." As soon as the words left her mouth she wished she hadn't spoke them. What if this guy was a rejected stepfather? Maybe that's why he takes and kills teen girls – because he was rejected by one when he was a stepfather. God, forgive me for saying such a thing.

"You're not a very sensitive girl, are you?"

"I know I shouldn't have said it like that. But he's not my step-father now, so none of it matters."

"It does matter. And it mattered a lot when he *was* your stepfather."

"What does it matter to you?" There I go again. That's Grandma in me. Shut your stupid mouth before it gets you killed.

"I'll ask the questions, Carly. Are you hungry?"

"A little, but I ate half that bread." She pointed to the remainder of the loaf on the table near him.

"I eat a lot of nature's bounty up here in these woods. But this time of year the pickings aren't as abundant, maybe some fir needle tea, or inner bark from a willow tree. I get some fish from downstream. There aren't any up here in the pools under the falls. I eat some beaver and raccoon meat, and deer and elk. I have some dried venison. Would you like some?"

"Maybe later," she answered, wondering where he kept the food. She always loved smoked venison. Her grandpa and her step dad used to make some in the fall after they got their deer.

Suddenly she remembered the story of Hansel and Gretel. How the wicked witch fattened them up before she was going to eat them. Maybe that's what he did to his girls—fattened them up before killing them. Surely he doesn't eat them.

"I'm going to leave you alone now," said the man. "There are some teen adventure books in the top drawer of the dresser."

"Where are you going?"

"I've got a few errands to run."

Is he actually going to hike out to the truck and go to town… or maybe *errands* to him means doing something out there in the woods? At least he's going to leave me alone, for now. I can't escape tonight, but if he's still gone in the morning, I've got to find a way out then.

9

The Creature

After the man left, Carly opened up the top drawer and found a dozen teen adventure books. She skimmed through them and picked out one called, Wild and Alive, about a couple of teenage girls who got lost in the woods for several weeks and how they survived. She was an avid reader and loved stories that took place in nature.

She stretched out on the cot, glad to still be alive. She did her best to relax and read by the light of the oil lamp on the table near the head of the cot.

Finally she was overcome by fatigue and fell off to sleep with the oil lamp still burning.

Two hours later, she dreamed she and Jeff were skimming along in a small row boat on one of the local ponds in the Roseburg area. It was late March. She was happy. Her basketball team had won the state championship. Everything was going great in her life. As Jeff continued to row the boat, she lay in the front, half asleep, with her left arm dangling partly over the side. She felt the cattails rubbing on her arm as they glided along. But something wasn't right.

She startled from her sleep. The oil lamp was out. It was pitch black. Suddenly, she felt something rub against her left arm.

She screamed.

It jumped and then came down on her legs.

She screamed again.

It jumped off the bed.

She panicked.

She cried and balled herself up in a fetal position under the sleeping bag. What was it, a wild animal? She wanted to look, but was too scared.

As she lay there under the sleeping bag, she felt the animal jump back onto the bed. She was too afraid to move. God, help me, she prayed. It walked around on the cot just above her head. Was it getting ready to bite her?

Then she heard a familiar sound—purring. What wild animal purrs? A wildcat? Cougar? Bobcat? She didn't know. Do raccoons purr? She didn't think so.

This animal wasn't big enough to be a cougar or bobcat. Maybe it was a young one. Not in the first week in February. What other wild animal purrs? She couldn't think of any. *Was it possible?*

Then she heard the animal meow. *It was a cat*—but not a wild-cat. She lifted the bag. It meowed again. She reached out for it in the darkness. It licked her arm with its raspy tongue. She loved cats. Thank God, it's a cat—a regular housecat. I'm not alone. She rolled back the bag and the cat rubbed up against her face, purring. She said out loud, "Thank you, God. I'm not alone. Where did you come from, little fella?"

She caressed the cat as it snuggled up against her.

She was fine—for now.

She fell asleep.

Thursday, two days missing—

Carly awakened to the smell of biscuits and gravy. For a few seconds she thought she was at her grandma's house for some holiday. She opened her eyes. He was sitting at the table, wearing that silly old man's mask.

She felt for the cat. Nothing. She looked around the lighted room. No cat. She realized she had never seen the cat. It had been too dark. She didn't even know what color it was. If he found the cat, did he do to it what he did to mice and girls? You can't think that way, Carly. It'll drive you insane. He hasn't killed you yet. Maybe he won't. He's just waiting for the right time. He hasn't even laid a hand on me, at least not to... He must have carried me into this cot the first night. If he hasn't done *that* to me yet, maybe he won't. God, don't let him do that.

"It's time for your breakfast, young lady."

'Young lady,' what's with that? That doesn't sound like the words of a killer. Why does his voice sound familiar?

"I baked you some biscuits and gravy outside in my Dutch oven."

What is it, cat meat? Stop it, Carly.

"I'll go out and let you get up and take care of business, put on some clean clothes, eat your breakfast, and then I want you to come outside by the pool. It's a beautiful day out."

"What time is it?" she said, wiping the sleep from her eyes.

"Is that the first thing you think about every day? Relax. There's no time schedule up here. I'll see you after a bit."

'After a bit,' was one of her ex-stepfather's favorite sayings. She always liked the way he said that.

When Carly came out near the pool after 'taking care of business,' putting on clean clothes, brushing her hair, and eating her fill of biscuits and gravy, the man was sitting on a small boulder watching some rock sparrows flit around at the other side of the pool bathing themselves.

Why won't he take that stupid mask off? And those gloves? That's a good sign isn't it? Killers only keep their faces hidden when they aren't going to kill. But his voice is familiar. Where have

I heard it before? Maybe that's why he won't take the mask off, because I'd know who he is.

"Sit down over here," he pointed to a boulder near him.

"What are you going to do to me?"

"Time will tell."

"Now *you're* using time," she said.

"It doesn't mean the same thing for me that it does for you."

"I don't understand. I don't understand any of this. Please, mister, can you just let me go home. I'm not like those other girls." Crap, there I go again. *Grandma*. Stop.

"What other girls?" he asked.

"The ones whose clothes you kept."

"Oh, I see. They didn't need them."

She was trembling again.

"Tell me more about your stepfather."

"Ex-stepfather," she corrected.

"Ex-stepfather; did you like him?"

"I don't understand what difference any of that makes. Can we just move on to some other subject?"

"You're good at that, aren't you?" he said.

"Good at what?"

"Stuffing things away, controlling the conversation so it stays away from things you don't care to think about."

"Think about? I'm lost."

"I bet you've shoved all thoughts of your stepfather aside for a long time, or tried to."

"Why should I ever think about him again? He's history. Gone. Ex-whatever. Life goes on. What is it with your interest in my fathers?"

"What if I told you *this* is all about your fathers, or rather, your stepfather?"

"Now I'm *really* lost," she said.

"He was your father for eight years."

"My mom left him. I had nothing to do with it. And he was never *my* father."

"That's what they all say."

"All who?"

"All the other ex-step kids."

"You don't know anything about me, about my life, or anything else."

"Are you sure of that?" he asked.

"I don't know. Your voice has something familiar to it. Maybe I've heard it before. But I can't place it."

"I guess there's no hiding some things, is there?"

"What? Am I right? I have heard your voice before?" She felt a glimmer of hope. It's harder for a killer to kill someone he knows, right?

"Not mine. But one like mine," he said. "I have to leave now for a while, so I want you to go inside until I'm gone. Then if you want to come out here and wash up you can. You'll find a wash cloth, soap, shampoo, and a towel to the left of the door, over on a little rock shelf. There's no point in trying to escape. You won't make it. When I get back I have some things to show you that you'll find interesting."

Are you serious? I just want out of here. Nothing you could show me would interest me. What did he mean when he said, "this is all about my stepfather?" Maybe that's what he's going to show me, some connection. I won't be here when he gets back, anyway.

"Okay," she answered.

10

Near Fall

When the man had been gone for twenty minutes, Carly went out and immediately searched for signs of the cable ladder. Nothing. He must have let it down, somehow, while she was inside, climbed up, then stowed it. That meant he had some way of releasing it from down here. No doubt, that's why he sent her inside, so she couldn't see how he released the ladder.

She searched the area near where the ladder had hung down the night they arrived. She looked under each bunch of spaghetti moss along the cliff face, not sure what she was looking for. Maybe a hidden rope or telescoping pole? There had to be something.

Nothing.

She then walked around the entire bedrock shelf that encircled the falls and pool. She stopped momentarily at the fire circle near the left canyon rock wall. This must be where he cooks.

She looked downstream and wondered. The stream turned a corner just beyond the immediate downstream pool preventing her from seeing any farther downstream. How many more falls were downstream? Were all the banks sheer cliffs, like these?

On the west side of the canyon, she held onto a two-inch-diameter tree root with her left hand and carefully leaned out over the cliff edge to get a good look at the pool below the downstream waterfall. How deep was the water in that pool? If it was deep enough, perhaps she could jump into it. Then once she landed safely there, maybe she could find a way out downstream.

As she leaned out at a forty-five degree angle, she observed that directly beneath the falls, twenty feet down, extending over twelve feet out to the main pool was nothing but sloped bedrock. The falling water deflected off that at an angle and sprayed out across the water in the pool and the bedrock shoreline.

The main pool was too far out—at least fifteen feet—and ran down the center of the canyon, in line with the stream. From either edge of the stream, from where she would have to jump, it would be at least twenty feet out and thirty feet down to reach the deep water. Impossible. Even if she was able to get a run at it, and jump from directly upstream—which she couldn't—the water was too shallow. She guessed no more than six or seven feet deep. She was screwed. She cried.

Then, as she pulled on the root with her left hand to bring herself upright, suddenly, the root broke free from the rock cliff. She screamed as she fell over the edge of the cliff, and slammed up against the left vertical rock face, while grabbing the root with her right hand. Her chin was even with the ledge she was just standing on. "God, help me!" she cried.

She dangled from the root, which was now holding steady. She thought of the words of her ex-stepfather, "Green tree roots are hard to break. You can use them, or strips of stringy, green tree bark, or sword fern to fasten things together."

Before she reached her teen years, they had built a couple shelters in the woods together, using those materials. That was before their relationship fell completely apart. "Everything you need to survive in the woods is out there. Just think things through and don't panic."

I bet he never hung from a cliff wall by a tree root. Is this a green tree root, or an old rotten one? "God, let it be green."

She dug the toe of one tennis shoe into the cliff on her left and the other into the rock face on the right. She reached ten inches up the root with her right hand and pulled herself up. Then she did the same with her left hand. At the same time, she used her feet to give her a little leverage. Twice more she moved each hand up the root, constantly praying, "God don't let this root break or come loose any further."

Finally she was high enough. She swiveled herself around and managed to sit on the ledge to the left, her feet dangling down. She continued to hold onto the root with both hands, while she lay down on her back, then scooted her way, inch-by-inch, back farther onto the ledge. She was safe.

She cried.

"Why me, God? Why is all this happening to me?"

After laying there for ten minutes, Carly got up to her feet and went to the water. She drank. Her head spun. She was so stressed. She drank some more.

She replayed, in her mind, her ex-stepfather's words about tree roots and bark. *Perhaps, she could make herself a rope.* There were no trees on this ledge in the canyon. She looked around for roots, but the only root of any size was the one she had dangled from. Maybe she could braid some small roots together to make a rope. But there weren't near enough small roots.

What about the moss? She could make a rope out of the moss. But it would take so much of the moss to have the strength to hold her weight. How could she pull down enough moss without him noticing the change? And if he caught her working with the moss, he'd know immediately what she was up to.

She looked around and saw there was plenty of stringy damp moss hanging throughout the cavern under the falls. She'd have to have a place to hide it, and she'd have to work where she could spot him coming before he spotted her. She'd work on it in the darkness of the cavern, where she could keep an eye on the side where he would toss the cable ladder down. When he came, she would see the ladder fall first, which would give her time to stash her work and get into the room, or out near the water where he wouldn't notice her until he'd gotten all the way down.

It could work. It had to work.

She found a nice crevice where she would hide her materials and the moss rope.

Just then she heard the cable ladder hit on the side of the rock face. She cringed. He was back. She went into the room and sat on the cot.

Three minutes later, he opened the door.

"How have you been, Carly?" he asked.

"I'm okay," Carly answered.

"Did you wash up?"

Oh no, he needs me to be clean for what he's going to do to me.

"Yes."

"Good. You should feel better then."

"How can I feel better when I'm still here? Why can't you just let me go home?" She started to cry.

"Please don't cry, Carly. You'll be okay."

"I'll never be okay as long as you keep me here away from my family and friends." She looked at her watch without him noticing. It was almost one.

"I told you before I left that I had some things to show you when I got back," he said. He pulled what looked like newspaper from a large pocket on the inside of his jacket. "Take a look at this." He handed her a single newspaper page, which had photos of two high school kids and a man, along with an article about a car accident.

She looked at it and said, "So?"

"Read the date in the upper right hand corner."

"September 16, 1998."

"Read the article title out loud."

She read, "**Astoria Girl Killed In Rollover Accident**"

"What does this have to do with me?" she asked. "I mean why would a teenage girl dying in a car crash over eleven years ago be of particular interest to me? It's sad, for sure. But it has nothing to do with me."

"Read the article out loud now."

She read, "**Astoria teenager Susan Hope Fitzgerald, 16, was killed just after midnight early Saturday morning in a fiery crash on the Astoria-Megler Bridge. The driver of the car she was riding in, Astoria star quarterback Bryan Russell, 17, is listed in serious condition at Columbia Memorial Hospital.**

A third victim in the crash, believed to be Edward Don Bradley, 36, reportedly jumped off the 200-foot-high bridge with his clothes on fire. Bradley's vehicle was the second one involved. At press time late-Saturday evening, Bradley's body had not yet been recovered. U.S. Coast Guard vessels and aircraft have been searching the Columbia River estuary and the Pacific Ocean since five a.m. Saturday morning. Clatsop County Sheriff's deputies, Oregon State Police and Washington State Police have also been involved in the search.

Coast Guard spokesman, Lieutenant Bill Ryder, said the search was delayed initially because there was confusion regarding the people involved in the accident. The police didn't learn that Bradley had jumped off the bridge until almost five Saturday morning when they were able to interview Bryan Russell. The outgoing tide from eleven Friday night until about five-thirty Saturday morning, which reached nearly four knots by 2 a.m., likely washed Bradley clear out to sea. The Coast Guard is not optimistic about recovering his body.

Oregon State Police and local law enforcement said alcohol was involved in the accident, though they wouldn't give any

other details. Neither Fitzgerald or Russell were wearing seatbelts."

"That's really sad. Did they ever find the man's body?" asked Carly.

"No."

"How sad."

"What happened to the Russell boy that was driving the one car?"

"I'll let you read that for yourself, if you really want to know. I have other clippings."

"Yes. I'd like to see them. But I still don't understand why you're showing me."

"You'll find out soon enough," he said. "But I'm hungry right now; how about some lunch?"

"Yes, I *am* feeling a little hungry."

The man went outside for a minute and returned with a backpack. He opened it and pulled out some oranges, a bag of potato chips, a loaf of wheat bread, a jar of peanut butter, a jar of grape jelly, and a half-gallon carton of milk, and set all of it on the table. "I hope you like peanut butter and jelly sandwiches. I'll let you make your own."

As he was placing the food on the table, Carly thought, he must have gone to the store. That means we aren't nearly as far away from civilization as I thought we were. She felt her spirits lift. If we're not that far out in the boonies, then maybe someone *will* find me. Or at least when I escape, it won't be that far to people.

She sat on the cot to eat, while he ate sitting at the table with his back to her.

After they had eaten lunch, he handed another newspaper clipping to Carly. She noticed the date was September 17, 1998, then read the article out loud, "**Man Still Missing After Astoria-Megler**

Bridge Accident" (a photo of each of the three accident victims accompanied the article)

"Police reported that long-time Astoria resident Edward Don Bradley was still missing, and his body has not been recovered, following the fiery two-car crash early Saturday morning, September 15th, which killed sixteen-year-old Susan Hope Fitzgerald and seriously injured seventeen-year-old Bryan Allen Russell. According to Russell, the man believed to be Edward Bradley jumped from the 200-foot-high Astoria-Megler Bridge while his clothes were on fire. U.S. Coast Guard vessels are continuing to search the Columbia River estuary and the Pacific Ocean for Bradley, but said the search would be called off in a day or so.

Russell, the Astoria star quarterback, remains in serious condition at Columbia Memorial Hospital with numerous broken bones, contusions, lacerations, abrasions and a punctured lung and liver. Police have interviewed Russell to get the details of the accident, but are not releasing those details at this time, pending the conclusion of their investigation. Oregon State Police spokesman, Captain Brock Riggs, admitted there are discrepancies between Russell's version of the accident and what law enforcement investigators have determined. He also said that alcohol was definitely a factor in the accident.

Captain Riggs was asked if any charges would be filed in the accident, but said that wasn't his call.

When Astoria High School varsity head football coach Frank Milton was asked about the accident and his team's loss of its star quarterback, he said, "Of course losing Bryan is a huge setback for our team. But far more important than our football team is that we all hope and pray for Bryan's speedy and complete recovery. All of our hearts go out to the families of Susan Fitzgerald and Eddie Bradley, and our prayer is that they will find God's grace and mercy during their time of loss and

sadness."

After reading the article, Carly asked, "What did the police investigation determine?"

"I'll let you read about that later."

"I still don't get what this has to do with me, or why you think it should be a big deal to me."

"I didn't say it would be a big deal to you. I said you would find it interesting."

"Well I think anyone would, don't you? Why is this article so important to you, anyway?"

"The girl that was killed, Susan Fitzgerald, was my daughter."

"Oh no!" said Carly, while her mind went into overdrive. "I'm so sorry. After nearly a minute of silence, Carly said, "I can't replace your daughter."

"No one could ever replace my daughter. Or the other daughter I lost."

"You lost two daughters?" she said. "I'm so sorry. What happened to the other one?"

"I'll explain it all to you later."

11

To the Heart

"**Right** now I want you to tell me more about your stepfather."

"That's it, isn't it? Either one or both of the girls you lost were your stepdaughters."

"I appreciate how you're trying to make the connection, but you're coming to the wrong conclusions.

"So the girls weren't your stepdaughters?"

"No, they weren't."

"Is your last name, Fitzgerald?"

"No."

"Then what is it, and why didn't the Fitzgerald girl have the same last name as you?"

"I can't tell you my last name. But I will tell you my first name, and if you want to call me by that, you can."

"That sounds like a deal." She was feeling much better. It's harder to kill someone if you tell them your name, right?

"My name's Warden."

"Is that like prison warden?"

"That's right."

"That's ironic, don't you think?" she said. "You're holding a girl hostage, yet your name's Warden. What kind of a warden would do something like that?"

"You're making too much of the name. I wouldn't have told you if I thought it would be such a big deal to you."

"I'm just being a normal teenager. Don't you know that?"

"Let's get back to your stepfather."

"Ex-stepfather."

"Okay. Tell me more about him. What did you think of him?"

"When my mom was dating him, and after they got married, I really liked him. He played with me all the time."

"Did you ever love him?"

Carly hesitated, thought for several seconds, started to say something, then stopped.

He gave her some time, then said, "Well, *did you* ever love him?"

Suddenly, she burst into tears. "Yes, when they first got married, I loved him with all my heart."

Tears welled up in Warden's eyes, then spilled down his cheeks inside the old man mask. He hadn't expected this. His heart went out to Carly. He put his head down, so she couldn't see his wet eyes through the mask.

He got up and walked outside.

Carly didn't know why. Was she getting to him? If she *was* getting to him, he wouldn't kill her, right? But her feelings were real. She didn't expect them to come out like that. She'd stuffed them away since her mom left Ken for the last time. She knew she was an expert at manipulation. But she wasn't crying to manipulate him. She was crying because she remembered the love she once felt for her stepfather. And because she felt so vulnerable right now. She wanted her stepfather, her ex-stepfather, to rescue her. She knew if he could he would. Had he even heard about her being kidnapped? Probably not. She hadn't heard anything about him in months. And he hadn't talked to her in nearly two years. Her mom's bogus restraining order made sure of that.

In a few minutes, Warden came back inside the room and sat down. "Why did you cry?" he asked her.

She had gotten a grip and wiped her face off. "I don't know. I didn't know I would. No one has ever asked me that question. No one ever seemed to care about what I felt inside about my stepfather."

"When you say no one cared, who are you talking about?"

"My family, Mom, Grandma, Grandpa, Aunt Maggie, my two older brothers."

He waited for her to say more, but when she didn't, he said, "Don't you have an older sister?"

"Yes."

"Why didn't you mention her just now? Was she different?"

"Yes. She was always neutral in the situation, in the problems between Mom and my stepfather."

"So she never took sides against him?"

"No. But she never stuck up for him either. She just always kept her mouth shut when everyone said bad things about him, or to him."

"How did all the family conflicts, the attacks against your stepfather, make you feel?"

"I was torn. Here were these people—my family—who I loved, and who had loved me since I was a baby. Yet they verbally ripped my stepfather to pieces."

"That must have been very hard on you, to be caught in the middle. One side of you loved him and knew that he must have loved you. But then all these other people that you love were trying to tear him down in your eyes, and they were trying to break up his and your mom's marriage. Did you ever try to tell anyone how you felt about that?"

"No. You'd have to understand how things work in our family. If you ever tried to go against what Grandma, Aunt Maggie, Mom, or my oldest brother Darren said, you were asking to get your ears burned."

"Did your family's opinion of your stepfather affect your feelings for him?"

"Of course."

"So what'd you do? Did you withdraw from him, *or reject him?*"

She broke down crying again. "Yes. Yes."

"And how did you do that?"

"When Mom married Ken," she said through tears, "I called him, "Dad." I didn't have a dad anymore because... well... you know... what the gang did to him in prison. I wanted a dad so bad. And Ken loved me so much."

"Then less than a year into their marriage, Grandma was over at our house one day and she really jumped down Dad's throat. Said some horrible things. It tore me up. This person I loved so much, Grandma, was ripping the shreds out of my dad."

"What did your mom do?"

"She didn't seem to know what to do. I think she was caught in the middle, too, that first time. Up until that day, I had never seen her even argue with my stepfather. They seemed so much in love. But something changed that day. Mom actually half took Grandma's side, even though nothing Grandma said about my stepfather, or to him, was true. When I went to bed a little while after the fight, I cried myself to sleep."

"What changed that day between your mom and stepfather?"

"It just seemed like they were never as close after that. Oh, things went okay for close to another year. But then the real big blowup happened with my family and stepfather."

"What happened?"

"It was Christmas. Everyone was at Grandma's house. Grandma was upset at my stepfather for something; who knows what. Then my stepfather had asked me about something, or told me to do something. That's when Grandma really got mean and said a horrible thing to him. Right there in front of everyone. Something a kid should never have to hear from her grandparent, or anyone."

"What'd she say?"

"Grandma said to him from across the room, 'Until you get *your act* together, you have no business saying anything to her.' Then she walked across the room and stood right in his face and said, "And furthermore, my blood runs through her, and yours never will.'"

"That's terrible. How did that make you feel?"

"Terrible, even though I wasn't sure what she meant. It was obvious it was pretty bad."

"What did your stepfather say in response?"

"He said, 'At least I'm not a gossip.' Since I was so young, I didn't really know what a gossip was, but I figured it must not be something good. Of course, after I got older and figured out what it was, and knew more about Grandma, I knew he had been right."

"She's a gossip?"

"The worst kind. She claims to be this super-spiritual person, then she turns around and tears people up behind their backs with her gossip. She spends half her time on the phone to Aunt Maggie, Mom, or my brothers. And believe me she isn't saying good things about the people she talks about."

"You seem to have a lot of insight into your family. Since you remember what was said, it must have been very traumatic for you that day."

"That day was the beginning of the end of my mom and step-fathers' marriage."

"And how did that affect you?"

"I grew more and more distant to him. Most the time I rejected him when he tried to show me affection."

"How did he do that?"

"He'd hug me or try to give me a kiss on the cheek or forehead."

"What'd you do to reject him?"

"I'd turn my head away when he tried to kiss me, or I'd get all stiff when he hugged me."

"You said that during the first year of the marriage you called him "Dad." What happened to that?"

"After that first argument that Grandma started between Mom and Ken, I quit calling him Dad."

"That must have hurt him," said Warden.

"It did. It really did. But in some ways, I was glad it hurt him—especially later in their marriage."

"Why?"

"Because I had listened to my relatives too much. And because of my rejection of him, he had mostly quit trying to show me affection."

"It sounds like a vicious, cycle," he said. "You hurt him by rejecting him because you felt an allegiance to your marriage-wrecking relatives. So he withdrew from showing you affection or taking an interest in you and your activities because you were rejecting him. Pretty sad."

"Looking back now, I must have hurt him as much as he hurt me."

"I'm sure you did."

"Did your daughters ever reject you?" she asked.

"The situation with my daughters wasn't anything like your situation with your stepfather. I'll tell you about it later. Right now, I'm going to go sit out in the woods for awhile. I'll bring you something for dinner, then leave you alone for the night. Are you getting any good reading in?"

"Yes. I read over half a book yesterday." She almost wanted to tell him she didn't want to be left alone again tonight. But the idea of the masked man staying anywhere near her for the night wasn't exactly comforting either—even if he showed her a caring human side today.

12

The Students

Two days missing, Thursday, Feb 4th—

Roseburg Girl Still Missing

Roseburg Police, Oregon State Police, and the Douglas County Sheriff Departments are still searching for missing Roseburg teen Carly Cantwell, and are asking for any information that the public can give that could help solve the case.

Cantwell, a sixteen-year-old junior, went missing Tuesday evening following the conclusion of her Roseburg High School varsity girls' basketball game. She is five-feet seven-inches, medium-build, has shoulder-length brown hair, and was last known to be wearing blue jeans, a pink, long-sleeve shirt, her black Roseburg High jacket, and white, high-top tennis shoes.

(two photos included)

The staff and students at Roseburg High School were taking Carly

Cantwell's disappearance very hard. Class time on Wednesday had mostly been spent talking about what Carly means to the students, students expressing their concern that the perpetrator is still out there on the loose, and speculating about why *she* was taken, and what might have been done to her. Many students were taking advantage of the group counseling sessions being offered.

In the hallway near some lockers Thursday afternoon, just after school let out—

"It couldn't have happened at a worse time for the girls' basketball team," said one girl.

"Yeah, with them going to Sheldon Friday night," said another. "If Sheldon wins, they'll pull even with us."

"Is that all you girls can think about—the basketball team?" another girl piped up. "Who cares about basketball at a time like this?"

"Life goes on. So does the basketball season."

"You guys are heartless."

"It couldn't have happened to a nicer girl," said another girl, sarcastically. "I guess she's *really* the center of attention now, isn't she?"

"I can't believe this. What kind of girls are you, anyway? Who cares what kind of girl she is or isn't? She's a human being. And no matter how jealous any of you are of her, she didn't deserve this."

"We're not jealous of her now." A few girls chuckled.

"We need to pray for her, for her safety and return," said the girl who had stuck up for her.

In the girls locker room, Carly's clique, *the in girls*—

"Can you believe this? Why would anyone take Carly?"

"You couldn't know a nicer girl."

"We're screwed if she isn't back by Friday night. We barely beat Sheldon last time… and that was at home. They haven't lost a game on their home floor in two years."

"Yeah, they tore us apart up there last year."

"Come on girls, the game doesn't mean anything. I'd forfeit the rest of the season to have her come back safe and sound."

"Me too."

"I don't even know why we have to practice tonight. You'd think coach Hollister would be more concerned."

"Don't you girls get it? He already gave us last night off. He told my dad that basketball practice will help get our minds off things for a while, at least partly."

"Yeah, that's probably true. What else would we do? Sit around at home and stew over it."

"Yeah, I think coach Hollister and your dad are right."

"Let's do it for Carly."

In the boys locker room—

"The police aren't doing any good finding her," said Jeff, Carly's boyfriend. "I think some of us guys should go looking for her."

"Where you going to look?" said another basketball player. "She could be anywhere."

"We don't even know if she's still alive," said another.

Jeff immediately shoved the kid up against his locker and held him there. "Don't you dare say that!"

"It's true," said Jeff's best friend, Rich, the six-foot seven-inch starting center, "and you know it is."

"You guys... you can't talk that way," said Sam Welker—the undefeated varsity 189 pound wrestler and team captain who took sixth in state at 171 last year—from the other side of the room. "And the last thing we need to do is fight with each other."

"What do you suggest?" another basketball player asked.

I think Jeff's right," answered Sam, "maybe we should look for her ourselves. At least we'd be doing something."

"Got any ideas about where to start?"

"How about if we go door to door to all the neighbors surrounding the high school and ask if any of them saw anything, maybe even the perpetrator's vehicle, around the time she would have been taken."

"I'm sure the police have done that already."

"Well we can't be sure of that. Do you have a better idea?"

"No."

"Okay then, tonight after our practices are over, we'll all meet over at the Safeway parking lot, divide up in twos and canvass the whole area. Between varsity and JV basketball players and wrestlers, that should give us at least twenty-five teams of two. If you're in, yell, 'I'm in,' on three. One. Two. Three."

"I'm in!" they all yelled in unison, then clapped their hands.

The Klamath County Sheriff's Department had still been unable to make contact with Carly's ex-stepfather, Ken Roderick. He hadn't come home yet. Douglas County Sheriff's Lieutenant Bond Hampton was growing more interested in him as a suspect by the hour. Thursday afternoon, he put out a state-wide APB (All Points Bulletin) on Roderick's vehicle, a brown 1993 Ford pickup, Oregon license plate CMS998.

The wrestlers and basketball players back at the Safeway parking lot, 8:30 pm—

"Did anyone get any information that could help us find Carly?" asked Sam Welker.

All the teams, except two, said nobody they talked to saw or knew anything. And almost all of them said the police had already questioned them. But two teams said they might have something.

"What'd you guys find out?" Jeff Lydle asked the remaining pair of two-man teams.

"We talked to a guy on Fern Street, who was out walking his dog at a little after nine Tuesday night, that said he saw an old pickup drive out of Cherry Lane."

"He did? What'd he tell you about the truck or passengers?"

"He said the truck was a brown mid-eighties Ford. He said he's a mechanic and knows his trucks. From where he was—which he said was about forty yards—he could only see one person in the truck. But he said he couldn't be sure."

"So he didn't get a good look at the driver?"

"No."

"Did he get a license plate number?"

"No."

"Did you ask him if the police had talked to him?"

"Yes. He said they came to his house a couple times on Wednesday, but he didn't answer the door."

"Why?"

"He said he and the police don't get along too good. He said he heard about Carly's disappearance on the news. But he didn't want to get involved and figured the truck he saw probably had nothing to do with her disappearance anyway."

"A local high school girl gets kidnapped, and he doesn't want to get involved? What kind of guy is he?"

"He was one of those throwbacks to the sixties, a hippie-type guy, long straggly hair, you know."

"So why did he *tell you* what he saw?"

"He said his conscience has been bothering him over it. Said he was even thinking about contacting the police after all, but we got there first."

"Is he still going to the police?"

"Yeah. He said he was going to call them as soon as we left."

Jeff then turned to the other team and asked for their information.

"It was an old lady that lives on Dennison Street. She said she saw a bright-green, late-model Camry speed by her house shortly after ten. She told the cops about it, but they didn't take her seriously. We got the feeling she probably calls the cops on a regular basis. You know how those old, busy-body batties can be. Do you think it could have been the kidnapper?"

"Any of you guys know anyone with a green late-model Camry?" asked Jeff.

"Yeah, Trent Summer's oldest brother owns one."

"Where's he live?"

"On Dennison Street."

"So much for that doing us any good," Sam said. "But I think that brown pickup definitely has possibilities. What do you guys think?"

"You're right."

"Now we just have to talk to the police about it so they can get right on it, even though we can't," said Jeff. "We have a home game tomorrow night against Sheldon, so we can't get out to the woods before Saturday. How about you wrestlers?"

"We have a meet at South Eugene tomorrow night. It's a three-way duel with them, Sheldon and us. But we don't have a tournament this Saturday because we have districts next weekend. So we can help you out Saturday."

"That's great," said Jeff. "I'm gonna call Jed Walker's dad (sheriff deputy) on my cell phone now and tell him what we found out. How about we all meet here with our cars and full tanks of gas at nine Saturday morning? I'll have maps of all the forest roads within a hundred miles of Roseburg. We'll start close and work out."

"Carly was probably taken a lot farther away than that," said one kid.

"But if she wasn't, and the kidnapper actually has her somewhere out in the woods in Douglas County, we can't possibly find her if we don't get out there, can we?" said Kyle.

"That's true."

"With the new information the police get on the truck, they'll probably put out an APB to stop every mid-eighties brown Ford pickup. But I bet they won't get out in the woods looking—at least not much."

"I think he's right. It's up to us to do that."

13

Happy

That evening in the room in the cavern under the falls—after Warden had returned with some food for Carly and left again to sleep in the woods during the night—Carly stretched out on the cot and did some more reading.

While she read, out of the corner of her eye, she saw movement near the end of the cot. The cat. Her heart leapt with joy.

"It's just you," she said to the cat as it jumped up on the cot and began rubbing itself against her, purring. "I was worried that something happened to you. Where did you go, and how did you get back in here?"

With the room lit up by the oil lamp, she saw the cat was a stocky, short-haired, gray and white tom. A very affectionate tom. She rubbed its head right behind the ears and scratched under its chin and just in front of its tail. She loved cats and knew just where they liked to be rubbed most.

He flopped down on his back. She scratched his chest and belly gently, while he grabbed her with his paws and licked her wrist with his raspy tongue. She giggled. She hadn't laughed or giggled in over two days. She said, "Thank you, God, for bringing this cat back to me."

"I'm going to call you 'Happy,' because you're the only thing that's made me happy since I was taken."

She got up and looked around for how *Happy* could have gotten in, since both the outside door and the bathroom door were closed. There it was: a loose board in the corner to the left of the dresser.

"I wonder if *he knows* about you. Maybe that's what he meant when I told him about the mice, and he said they don't live long. They don't live long because of you, Happy. Do you eat those little mice, big fella? I bet you do. What else do you find to eat out here in the woods?"

She smiled as she continued to talk to Happy, while she stroked him. "How long have you been living here? Or *do you* live here? Where do you live? Do you live with people? If you do, how far away do they live? I wish you could talk to me. I wish you could tell me where I am. I wish you could help me escape, and lead me to safety. If you were a dog, I bet you could help me. And I bet you would.

"Some people say cats aren't near as smart as dogs, because you really can't teach them much. But other people say cats are much smarter, because they only do what they want to do and not what people try to make them do. What about you, Happy? Are you smarter than a dog? I bet you are. I'm gonna come back and get you to be my cat, whenever I get out of here. Would you like that? *If* I ever get out of here."

"God, please let me get out of here. I can't replace his daughters anymore than the other girls could. Please don't let him hurt me."

Happy stood up suddenly, and froze, head high, ears alert, his face turned toward the outside wall. "What is it boy?" she whispered. "Is something out there?"

She heard a noise. She wished she had a dog—a *big* dog.

The door opened. She screamed. Happy startled.

Warden walked in.

"It's only me, Carly," he said. "It's okay."

"You scared me; I thought you were somebody else."

"I see you've made friends with the cat." She noticed he didn't say, my cat, or call it by name. Just: *the cat*.

She rubbed Happy on top of his head and on his neck, as he arched his neck up.

"He obviously likes you. He's a good cat. He keeps the mice in check around here for me."

"Yes. He's a good boy. I named him, *Happy*, because he's the only thing that's made me happy since you took me."

"I'm glad you like him. I don't want you to be unhappy here, Carly."

"What else could I be?" she said defiantly. "You're a stranger who has taken me far away from my family, friends, school, boyfriend, sports, everything. For what? To replace your daughters? To kill me? For what? What do you expect me to feel?"

She cried partly out of relief that it was him and not something or someone else that came through the door and partly out of despair because *it was him* and he was keeping her prisoner.

He stood just inside the door, making no move toward her, though he wanted desperately to go to her and take her in his arms to comfort her. To take away her pain. *The pain that he was causing her.* But he was doing all this *for her.* He didn't expect her to understand that yet.

"I just came back to check on you one last time tonight. I'll see you in the morning." He turned and left, shutting the door behind him.

14

Game Day

The next morning, Friday, three days missing—

After Warden and Carly had eaten fried fish, potatoes, and oranges, and drank milk for breakfast, he said, "Carly, we have some more ground to cover today."

"I don't want to cover anymore ground with you. Today is the biggest game of my team's season. We're playing Sheldon. They're only one game back of us in league. We only beat them by one point on our home court last time. And that was because I made a three-point-shot at the buzzer."

"I saw that game. That was a great shot."

"You were there? Then you know how important I am to my team. You saw that they never would've won that game without me."

"You're a legend in your own mind, aren't you, Carly?"

She didn't answer. He was right. She did think very highly of herself. Or rather, she wanted everyone else to think highly of her despite what she really thought of herself.

"Don't you think your team has more going for it than just you? Don't you think they're capable of winning a big game without you? Do you think you're God's gift to mankind? Do you think you're better than everybody else? You thought you were better than your stepfather, didn't you? So much better that you could turn your nose up when he tried to show you love. There's so much you don't know, Carly."

"Stop!" she cried.

"Stop torturing me. You don't know what you're saying. Do you get off on psychologically torturing teen girls? Or is this just the foreplay to physically torturing them?"

"Have you always had such a big mouth, Carly? Who'd you get that from? Your mom? Your grandma? Your Aunt Maggie? Who? Tell me.

"Stop it! Stop saying those cruel things," she begged. "You're the crazy one here. Not me!"

"I'm going outside for a bit, to let you settle down," he said. "Then we'll talk some more."

Half an hour later, Carly came outside and sat on the boulder near the one Warden was sitting on, at the east side of the pool. He was watching birds bathe at the far edge of the pool, near the west side of the falls, chirping and singing their songs.

"You're right, you know," Carly said to him.

"About what?"

"About me. About the things you said in there. It's all true. I'm all about me. I have been for as long as I can remember. Oh sure, sometimes I feel bad for other kids, that they don't get the breaks, that they can't do things as good as I can, that they get picked last for teams, that they don't get to go to everyone else's birthday parties like I do, that they aren't the homecoming queen, that they aren't the best at everything. Sure I feel bad for them sometimes. But I'm glad I'm not them."

"*Do you* get the breaks, Carly?"

"A lot of times it seems like it."

"So would you trade your life for any of your friends' lives?"

"What?"

"Would you trade the life you have, with everything good about it, for the lives of any other kids?"

She sat silently, contemplating his question, watching the *birds*, thinking how carefree they seemed. They didn't have to consider such things. They just had to eat and flit around and play. Their life was so simple. She often wished her life was more simple, without everyone's high expectations on her…her mom's and grandma's criticism…her mom's demands.

"Why are you asking me that?" she said.

"It doesn't matter why I'm asking. Just give me your answer."

She thought some more.

He waited.

She started crying.

She cries too much, he thought. It makes this too hard.

"Yes," she finally admitted. "Yes, I would trade my life for some other kid's in a heartbeat."

"Do you think any kids would trade their lives for yours, Carly? Do you think any kids would love to be you?"

"I hope not."

"Why's that, Carly?"

"They don't know *how hard* it is *to be me*. They don't know what really goes on inside me."

"What goes on inside you that they don't know about?"

"I'm just a scared little girl on the inside. I'm always supposed to be the best at everything.

"To be the leader.

"To never fail. To never quit.

"To never give up and say it's too much for me. That it's too much for any girl—for anyone."

"Why can't you tell anyone how you really feel?"

"I can't even let *myself* feel how I really feel. Can't you understand that?" she said. "Why do you do this to me? Why are you making me look inside myself? Please, just let me go back to my life. Take me back."

"Carly, what is it about some other kids that would make you want to trade your life for theirs? Why would you want *to be them*?"

She tried to speak, but choked up.

"Carly, tell me what you see in some of your friends' lives that you long for the most—that you don't have in your life, that you wished you did have."

She tried again. The words *still stuck* in her throat. It was too hard. Tears leaked down her cheeks and fell on the boulder between her legs.

"Carly?"

"I wish I had a dad!" she blurted out. "I wish I had a dad like other girls do. I wish I had a dad and mom in love with each other." The dam broke. She wept. Her whole body shook.

He couldn't take it. He moved over to her and engulfed her in his arms. There was so much he wanted to say to her. But he knew he couldn't. Not yet. This man, hiding under the mask that was soaked inside with his tears.

He felt her pain.

He felt his own pain.

Fathers.

Daughters.

Broken marriages.

Broken relationships.

Why did it have to be so hard?

15

The Daughters

He held her in his arms for a minute, then she suddenly stiffened, pulled away, and said, "Let go of me! Is that what you do, get the girls all emotional, make them vulnerable, so they need you to comfort them? I've heard about some of the tactics child molesters use to connect with their victims. You're not doing that with me. Get away from me."

He couldn't believe how she could go from being so hard to so soft and vulnerable back to being so cold and obnoxious. But then he put himself in her shoes and he understood.

"I'm sorry, Carly. I just felt compassion for you. I did what came natural as a father. Something I never got to do with my own daughters."

"Well I told you before: I'm not your daughter!" she said. Then thinking about what he just said, she asked, "Why didn't you get to hold your own daughters? You didn't molest *them* did you?"

"Would you drop it with the molesting accusations and thoughts? I would never hurt anyone."

"Then why didn't you get to hold your own girls? You said you would tell me about your daughters later. I'm listening."

"I guess now's as good a time as any," he said.

"When I was nineteen, I got a senior at Astoria High School pregnant. I had just moved to the area a few months earlier. I met her one day while I was at the beach near the end of the summer. I ran into her a few times after that, then one night she turned up at a party I was at. After she'd had too much to drink, I took advantage of the situation."

"That's when you got her pregnant, at the party?"

"That's right. No one else knew. I snuck her off to an empty bedroom.

"She came from a Christian home, and it was a one-time slip up for her. At least that's what she told me later. Her dad was an elder at a big church in town, but the girl said he had quite a temper. She said he would kill me if he ever found out I got her pregnant."

"Since you're not dead, he must not have found out, right?" Carly asked.

"That's right."

"So what happened, I mean with the pregnancy and everything?"

"The girl, Angie, and I agreed to never reveal to her parents or anyone that I was the father. I agreed to pay her $150 a month under the table for child support. No one ever knew she was getting it. She couldn't even tell her parents, because she knew her dad wouldn't give up until he figured out who she was getting the money from. Then he would still kill me. The year she had the baby was 1982. Things were a lot different back then. There weren't any DNA tests or anyway to prove paternity. So as long as she never revealed who the father was, it would never be known."

"Did you love Angie?"

"No. We hardly knew each other at the time I got her pregnant. It was a one-night thing. She resented me for getting her pregnant, but not enough to tell her dad and have me end up dead."

"Did you get to have visits with your daughter?"

"No. We agreed that it was best for me to just go on with my life as if I wasn't her father."

"And you did that. Just like that. Had no interest in being involved in your own daughter's life? How could you do that? How can any man do that? Girls need their fathers."

"It wasn't *just like that*." he said.

"If you never had anything to do with Susan Fitzgerald after she was born, why do you even speak as if you lost your own daughter in that accident on the bridge that day? I don't understand."

"I never said I didn't have anything to do with her?"

"So you did, but not as her father?" Carly asked.

"That's right. But you're getting a little ahead of me," he answered.

"Go on."

"Six months after Susan was born, Angie, her mother, married a good Christian man that had graduated in the class ahead of her."

"I bet his name was Fitzgerald."

"You're smart."

"Anyway, Mr. Fitzgerald and Angie had three more kids after he adopted Susan. They lived happily ever after, that is until Susan was killed in the accident."

"If he adopted Susan, why did you continue to give Angie child support?"

"Because I always felt it was my responsibility. Besides, although Fitzgerald was a great guy, he was not the greatest provider, worked low paying jobs."

"You said you were involved in Susan's life; in what way?"

"Not nearly like I would have liked, mostly from a distance. Angie was nice enough to let Susan accept me as that fun guy at the park. You know the grownup that likes to play on the merry-go-round, climb the monkey bars, go down the slide, swing, play his guitar and sing. That kind of stuff. You know the kind of guy kids are drawn to."

"So you got to play and talk with Susan and Angie at the park?"

"That's right. Not very often, maybe a couple afternoons a month, less as Susan got older and got busy with friends and other activities."

"Do you think Angie's husband ever suspected anything?" Carly asked.

"I'm sure he did. But since he loved kids, and I was an okay guy, I think he must have had some empathy for me. He never said anything to me, and Angie never said anything to me about him discussing me with her. I was always grateful to both of them for the role they let me play."

"What about when Susan got older? Did you still see her much?"

"Yes. As a matter of fact, I ended up coaching her in softball for a bunch of years. I just moved up with her grade each year. It was wonderful. She was such a good-natured kid, very coachable, a great team mate, and a pretty good player. I used to love to hear her bust out laughing over something that happened on the field or in the dugout. She had a contagious laugh."

"She sounds like she was a special girl."

"She was very special, though among her peers she was just your average girl—nothing like you. She had a couple friends that were real popular like you, but popularity was never important to her. Her parents and younger siblings loved her deeply. They had quite a family. She found so much of her happiness at home with them."

"Did she ever find out that you were her biological father?"

"No."

"That must have hurt, coaching your own daughter and knowing she didn't know that."

"Yes, it hurt deep inside me. But it had to be that way for every-one's sake."

"It seems so wrong," she said, "the two of you living in the same community, you coaching her and all that, and she didn't even get to know the truth about you, about her."

"Some things are better left alone. I was just thankful for what I did get with her."

"Tell me about your other daughter and your wife," said Carly. "You did get married, didn't you?"

"Yes. I got married two years after Susan was born, when I was twenty-two. I married a gal that had moved into the Astoria area the same summer I did."

"Are you still married to her?"

"That's a sad story," he answered.

"Your life has had a lot of sadness in it, hasn't it?"

"It wasn't always easy. That's for sure."

"What happened to your marriage?"

"My wife, Reeta, was beautiful. She had long, full, flowing black hair, and a dark complexion. She was half Indian, that is, native American. We were very much in love at one time. Then the tragedy happened."

"Tragedy?"

"Well, since Reeta and I both loved kids, we never used birth control because we wanted to have a child right away."

"Did you?"

"No. Not right away. Not at all. We tried for three years. Nothing. We both finally went to the doctor to see if either of us had a problem. It turned out *she was sterile*. Her eggs never matured in her ovaries."

"That's very sad. But you said you had another daughter, so did you adopt?"

"We did. Or, I should say, we almost did. The adoption was in the final stage. We had flown to Vietnam twice to meet, then later visit, the beautiful, little, dark-skinned Vietnamese girl we were adopting from an orphanage in Ho Chi Min city. Most American veterans still call the city *Saigon*, because that was its name until the communists from North Vietnam won the war in 1975 and took over the south.

"Anyway, two weeks before we were to fly over to pick up our four-year-old daughter, she was run over by a motorcyclist who was speeding by on the street outside the orphanage. Her death crushed us, and instead of pulling together during our heartache, we drifted apart. Two years later, she found someone else and divorced me. Neither of us ever had kids after that."

He saw tears trickle down Carly's face, as she stared at him with compassion, but said nothing.

16

Arrest

After receiving phone calls from Jeff Ryder (Carly Cantwell's boyfriend) and the hippie on Fern Street after 9 pm Thursday night, the Douglas County Sheriff Department's Lieutenant Hampton had driven over to talk to the hippie, Bennie Vinn, in person about the pickup he said he had observed on Cherry Lane.

Upon learning that the pickup Vinn observed was a mid-eighties Ford—which meant it was too old to be Carly's ex-stepfather's truck—Lt. Hampton asked Vinn if it could have been a newer truck. Vinn then told Hampton that he is a mechanic and knows the difference between the mid-eighties models and a 1993, a two-wheel-drive and four, and a half-ton and a three-quarter ton. "This truck is not the one you're already looking for. And like I told the wrestlers, it probably had nothing to do with the girl's disappearance."

At 10:38 Friday morning, Lt. Hampton received the call he'd been waiting for. An Oregon State trooper had Ken Roderick's eastbound truck pulled over on the Crater Lake Highway, ten miles east of Diamond Lake. The trooper had obtained Roderick's driver's license, vehicle registration, and proof of insurance without incident. He was currently awaiting backup from a Klamath County Sheriff deputy—who was about five minutes out coming from the east—before informing Roderick about his missing ex-stepdaughter and asking him what he knew about it. He told Roderick he pulled him over because his left tail light was flickering.

Five minutes later the Klamath County deputy pulled his squad car directly in front of Roderick's pickup. The state trooper, who was parked behind Roderick, then got out of his vehicle and cautiously approached Roderick's vehicle at the same time the deputy approached from the opposite direction, while Lt. Hampton and other law enforcement officials monitored their radios.

"Mr. Roderick, please step out of your vehicle," said the trooper.

"Is there a problem, officer?"

"Please, just step out of your vehicle, now." Both officers stood back several feet and had a hand on their holstered .38s, in case Roderick pulled anything.

"What's this about?" Roderick said, as he got out and stood next to his truck.

"Turn around and place your hands on the top of your vehicle," said the trooper.

Roderick complied reluctantly.

The sheriff deputy immediately stepped up and frisked him, finding no weapons.

"Your ex-stepdaughter, Carly Cantwell, is missing," the trooper said. "What do you know about that?"

"Carly's missing?" he said, seeming genuinely surprised. "How would I know anything about that?"

"She's been missing since shortly after her varsity basketball game at Roseburg High School on Tuesday night. Your ex-wife named you as a possible suspect."

"That'd be just like her. I don't know anything about it. I haven't seen Carly in over a year."

Both officers kept a close eye on Roderick, as he spoke, to read his non-verbal language and to ensure he didn't try anything.

"The Klamath County Sheriff's Department and the State Police have been attempting to contact you since Wednesday morning. Where have you been?"

"I went to Medford to see a woman I met several weeks ago through the Singlesworld internet dating site. We went out Monday afternoon and evening, then she let me sleep in her spare bedroom Monday night. We spent Tuesday together until around three. Since then I've been over toward the coast to scout some areas for the upcoming spring black bear season."

"So you don't have an alibi from Tuesday afternoon until now?" asked the trooper.

"No, unfortunately, I don't. But I'm not guilty of anything. I would never do anything to harm Carly. I loved that girl." He didn't add, *as hard as that was at times.*

Both troopers had looked into the cab and inside the canopy into the truck's bed through the windows and saw nothing suspicious. They noted a couple of unrolled sleeping bags, blankets, duffle bag, some food, and miscellaneous other items.

"Well, stay where you are. I've got to talk to the Douglas County Sheriff." The trooper walked back to his squad car, while the deputy stayed with the five-foot eleven-inch, medium built Roderick. Neither of the officers was sure whether he was telling the truth.

Over his radio where Roderick couldn't hear him, the trooper said, "Lieutenant Hampton, what do you think? He seems to be telling the truth, and so far we haven't spotted anything suspicious. Should we search his vehicle, or take him into custody?"

"He's our only suspect so far. I talked with a guy last night that lives in Roseburg not far from the high school who said he saw a brown mid-eighties half-ton, two wheel drive pickup leaving the area several blocks away from the school at about the time the Cantwell girl would have been taken."

"Yeah, I learned that over the radio this morning when I came on duty," said the trooper. "Roderick's truck is a four-wheel drive, three-quarter ton, with a brown canopy on it. It can't be the same one your witness saw, unless the description your witness gave isn't right."

"No that's not it, he didn't say anything about a canopy either," said Hampton. "The guy's a mechanic and was sure of his description."

"Where's that leave us?"

"We don't even know if the truck the witness saw has anything to do with the girl's disappearance. But if it does, either Roderick was driving a different truck. Or he didn't do it," said Hampton. "If only the witness could have gotten the plate number, or a physical description of the pickup's driver. He wasn't even sure if the driver was a male or not. I hate to let Roderick go. But right now, the only things we have on him are his ex-wife's suspicion, his not being home since it happened, and his having no alibi. You guys do a quick search of his vehicle to see if you find anything that could be the girl's. If you find anything suspicious, arrest him. If not, we have to let him go, for now."

"Okay, Lieutenant," answered the trooper. "I'll let you know before we cut him loose."

"I'll be listening."

The state trooper returned to Roderick's truck and talked to him some more, while the sheriff deputy searched his vehicle. Two minutes later, the deputy found something in one of the sleeping bags. He immediately returned to the driver's side of the truck and nodded at the state trooper. The state trooper stepped up behind Roderick—still standing with his hands on top of the truck—grabbed his right wrist and pulled it around to his back, while saying, "We're placing you under arrest for the possible kidnapping of Carly Cantwell."

As the trooper slapped a handcuff on him, Roderick objected, "I don't know what you're doing. I had nothing to do with her disappearance."

After the trooper quoted Roderick his Miranda Rights, the deputy said, "I just found a couple long blond hairs in one of your sleeping bags. What do you have to say about that?"

"I don't know where they came from. Those sleeping bags have been slept in by a number of people over the years. Even Carly slept in them back before her grandma tore her mom's and my marriage apart." The officers looked knowingly at each other; Roderick saw that and wasn't sure whether they did it because they were thinking, "tell us another one," or "another meddling mother-in-law does it again." He hoped it was the second reason. "Why would I take her anyway? What kind of supposed motive do I have? Doesn't a guy have to have motive to do a crime? Come on guys, I didn't do it."

"Look Roderick, a guy witnessed a suspicious brown Ford pick-up driving away from near your stepdaughter's school at the time she was taken. You're driving a brown Ford pickup, you haven't been home in days, you have no alibi, and a couple of your step-daughter's hairs are in one of your sleeping bags."

"I didn't do it. I wouldn't hurt my own daughter."

"Deputy Mitchell is going to transport you to the Klamath-Douglas County line and turn you over to the Douglas County Sheriff's Department. If you are innocent, you can clear things up with them. We're just following orders."

"I'm being railroaded, and you guys know it. Carly's family did the same thing to me. Once my mother-in-law turned against me, I couldn't do anything right. This is just one more thing I'm being blamed for that I didn't do. And while everyone's wasting their energy on me, the real perpetrator is getting away with it. And my ex-daughter is going through hell, if she's even still alive."

"Knock it off, Roderick. Nothing you can say is going to change things right now. You'll get your chance to straighten things out in Roseburg."

Roderick continued to assert his innocence, but to no avail.

17

In Custody

At Douglas County Sheriff's Office, 2:00 pm, Friday—

"Roderick, we need to know what you've done with your ex-stepdaughter," said Lieutenant Hampton.

"I thought a guy was innocent until proven guilty. We're sitting here at your station, while whoever took Carly is getting away with it. You should have your men out there looking for the guy that took her, instead of harassing me. I told you, I don't know anything about it."

"The lab is testing the hair right now against the DNA we got from hair taken off her pillow at her home. When they come back as a positive match, you're in a world of hurt."

"What is it that you guys aren't getting?" said Roderick. "I already told you, Carly slept in those sleeping bags when we went camping."

"Where is your camp, Roderick? Is she still alive?"

"You're not listening to me Lieutenant. I haven't seen Carly in well over a year. My ex-wife sewed things up tight with her bogus restraining order. None of the things she accused me of ever happened. She used the restraining orders to shut me out of her life and to shut me out of Carly's life as well. You should be interrogating her, not me. The woman's got serious issues. And she drags that cord around with her everywhere she goes."

"What cord?"

"The umbilical cord connecting her to her mother, my ex-mother-in-law. She was never really married to me, because she was never able to cut the cord to her mom. They'd do anything to get me behind bars and keep me there, including accusing me of taking Carly. I didn't do it, no matter what you think you have on me. For crying out loud, get out there and find her before it is too late, *if it isn't already.*"

Local news stations—

Suspect in Custody in Missing Girl Case

Kenneth Dean Roderick of Chemult is being held by the Douglas County Sheriff Department as the prime suspect in the abduction of his ex-wife's daughter, Carly Rose Cantwell. Cantwell went missing Tuesday, February 2nd, some time after her varsity basketball game at Roseburg High School. She was believed to have been taken while in the school's southeast parking lot.

Roderick was arrested by the Klamath County Sheriff Department and Oregon State Police this morning on the Crater Lake Highway, ten miles east of Diamond Lake. Authorities have considered him a person of interest in her disappearance since Wednesday morning, but had been unable to determine his whereabouts.

When asked if he felt confident that the right person was in custody, Douglas County Sheriff Detective Bond Hampton said, "At this point we're not certain, but we're continuing our

efforts to determine that."

"What caused you to consider him a suspect?"

"I can't discuss that at this time."

"Have you found Carly Cantwell, or do you know where she is? Is she alive, Lieutenant?"

"No we have not found Ms. Cantwell. As would be expected, the suspect denies his involvement and denies having any knowledge of his ex-stepdaughter's whereabouts."

"What are your department and other law enforcement agencies doing to locate Ms. Cantwell? Is the FBI involved?"

"Yes, the FBI is involved. The FBI, along with our department, Roseburg Police and the Oregon State Police are taking every measure possible to locate Miss Cantwell. However, I can't discuss those details with you now. I have no more to say at this time other than we welcome any leads or clues the public can provide us. Even though we have a suspect in custody, the case is far from solved."

While Warden was away throughout the afternoon, Carly worked furiously gathering stringy moss and weaving it into rope. She was discouraged to find that the moss was more fragile than she thought it would be, and knew it was going to take a lot more of it to get enough strength to support her weight. Right now she wished she was one of the stick chicks that she'd sometimes made fun of instead of the meaty, athletically-built girl she was.

After working for what she thought must be a couple hours, she looked at her watch. It was almost four. It would be dark in less than two hours. After the talks she and Warden had had, she was no longer afraid that he planned to harm her right away. She was still at a loss about why he took her and what his ultimate plan was for her. But there was something good about him, something deeper. She just couldn't put her finger on it yet.

Just then she heard the ladder drop. She hustled to hide her work in a damp crevice, then sat on the west side of the pool, where he wouldn't see her until he got most the way down the ladder.

When he saw her sitting there, he asked, "How was your afternoon, Carly?"

"Boring and lonely."

"It doesn't have to be either, you know. Did the cat come around?"

"No. But I hope he does tonight, so he can snuggle with me and keep me company."

"He's very friendly, isn't he?"

"Yes, he is," she answered. "Most cats are, if you give them half a chance."

"People are too."

"Maybe so. And very few would ever kidnap someone. Only the worst would do that."

"So you still think I'm a bad guy?"

"I'm here, aren't I?"

Changing the subject, Warden said, "I've got some disturbing news for you, Carly. Your stepfather was arrested today and is being held for kidnapping you."

"What?" she said. "He'd never do anything like that. He's nothing like you. Why do they think he took me?"

"The reporters didn't get a reason from the police as to why he is the prime suspect."

"Why would they think *he* did it?" she asked.

"Why don't *you* tell me?"

"How would I know?"

"You said yourself that your mother's family was against him from early in their marriage and did everything they could to make him look bad. One of them, perhaps even your mom, surely told the police that he may have been the one who took you."

"That's absurd," she said.

"Why?"

"No one in my family would tell the police that."

"You said your mom got a restraining order against him to shut him out of your life."

"I don't remember telling you that."

"Did she?"

"Yes," Carly admitted.

"So if she thought he was enough of a danger to herself and you to restrain him from seeing you after she left him, why doesn't it seem reasonable that she would tell the police that he could have taken you."

"She may not have loved him anymore, but I can't believe she would believe that, let alone say that to the police."

"You've chosen to just pretend a lot of stuff isn't true about your family, haven't you, Carly?"

"What do you mean?"

"Like that. Like a lot of the bad things your relatives said and did to your stepfather to destroy his and your mom's marriage, and your relationship with him."

Here we go again with his psychological ploys. Why can't he quit messing with my head?

"I'm just curious, Carly. Did your *stepfather's family* interfere in the marriage, in your home and family?"

"Well, no, actually they didn't."

"Was he worse than your mom, more to blame for things?"

"I don't know. Maybe. Well, I guess not. Actually, I think she was more of the problem."

"Yet his family didn't interfere or attack her, right?"

"Yeah, that's right," she said.

"Did that ever strike you as odd that your mom's relatives did and his didn't?"

"I didn't give it much thought."

"But you sure lived with the drama of it, didn't you?"

"Yes, I did. And it was terrible."

18

Classmate Search

Shortly after school, Friday—

Jeff Lydle talking by cell phone to Sam Welker: "I talked with Joe's dad (a classmate's cop father), a little bit ago about the news report of Carly's ex-stepfather's arrest."

"Yeah, what'd he say?" asked Sam.

"He said the cops aren't convinced that her stepfather took her," Jeff answered. "He said, Carly's mom was the one who named him as a suspect. But he wasn't buying it. He said Carly's mom has a history of restraining orders and accusations against her ex's."

"Some example for Carly, huh?"

"I won't comment on that one," said Jeff. "The FBI, the OSP and the Douglas County Sheriff Department are all continuing to go about the case as if they don't have the proper person in custody."

"What are they doing?"

"Joe's dad said he couldn't get into that with me, but that it sounded like they had the bases covered pretty well."

"So we're still on for getting the guys out into the woods

tomorrow?"

"Yeah."

"Have you got a hold of the maps we'll need to pass out?"

"Yes," answered Jeff. "My dad's buddy at the forest service office gave me twenty-five copies of the Umpqua National Forest topographical maps."

"That's great. People are sure pulling together to find her, aren't they?"

"Well let's hope we can find her tomorrow. What do you think the chances are that she's still in Douglas County?" asked Jeff.

"I don't have a clue. But that's where we could do the most good, if she is."

"Good luck with your matches tonight. Kyle told me the 189 pounder from Sheldon has only lost two matches, and they were close decisions to two of the other top-ranked wrestlers in the state."

"Yeah, he's gonna be tough," Sam answered. "I beat him twice last year, including for the district championship. Both times I won by two points. I'm glad I've got him first tonight. Good luck in your game."

"Thanks. See you at Safeway in the morning."

Four days missing, Saturday morning, Safeway parking lot—

"I heard you stuck the Sheldon kid late in the third round with a guillotine," said Jeff. "That's great."

"Yeah, he was up by one at the time," said Sam. "I had to dig deep. I'm not looking forward to seeing him at the district meet next weekend. I heard you guys *and the girls* got the job done. Even without Carly, they did it."

"Both of our teams won by one point. Our JV guys won theirs too."

After dividing up into three-man-teams made up of wrestlers, basketball players and some other kids, including several of Carly's girl friends, everyone listened up for final instructions from Jeff Lydle.

"Does every team have at least one cell phone, a compass, a map and a full tank of gas in its vehicle?"

"Yes," each of the nineteen teams answered.

"We're gonna drive out every logging road and every spur in every drainage beginning with Little River, just this side of Glide. My team and teams two and three will take the Little River Road. You can see on the map here where I've assigned the other teams, farther up the North Umpqua Highway. Joe's dad told me this morning that they received two reports of brown pickups seen in these woods by recreationists yesterday. We can only hope one of them is our man. Apparently the FBI, Sheriff and OSP will also be in those areas today as well as elsewhere. If you run into any of them, be courteous and don't volunteer what you're doing out there. I'm sure they'll figure it out. But they can't openly support what we're doing, or they could be held liable if anything happens to any of us."

"Do you think something could happen to any of us?" asked Shelly, one of Carly's friends. "I mean we aren't in any danger are we?"

"Come off it, Shelly," said one of the wrestlers. "Carly's out there all by herself with some lunatic, and you're worried about yourself?"

"You guys, let's work together," said Sam.

They all broke up, got in their vehicles and headed out of town to the east, up the North Umpqua Highway.

On the Little River Road an hour and a half later, 10:50—

By cell phone, "Sam, I'm going to take my team, along with teams two and three, up to the headwaters here on Little River," said Jeff. "One of the pickups was seen out this way. Our teams have driven out every road out here so far and only seen just two vehicles. I think they may have been FBI teams, but I'm not sure. I'll keep in touch with you guys if I can. In the steep country out here we may lose cell service."

"Alright," Sam answered. "If I can't contact you, hopefully I'll still be able to stay in contact with the other teams. Good luck."

Teams one, two and three stood around the hood of Jeff's pickup looking at a map. Jeff said, "Okay, I have a funny feeling about this area. Little River, which isn't much more than a creek now, broke away from the road a couple miles back. As you can see here on the map, it's below us in that steep canyon back there about three-quarters of a mile to the west from here. We're gonna hike into that canyon. I was in there a long time ago with my dad. Don't ask me why, I just feel like this is where we need to look. That one brown truck was reported out this way."

Jeff tried to call Sam on his cell phone but had no service. However, his GPS was picking up several satellites and tracking well.

After each team member put on his backpack containing water, some food and an extra sweatshirt or two, Jeff said, "Let's go," then led the way into the forest of second-growth Douglas Firs with some cedar and western hemlock mixed in.

They had hiked twenty minutes when they began hearing waterfalls. "Carly!" Jeff yelled. "Carly!" He and the other team members, that included two girls, Kelly and Mandy, began yelling Carly's name regularly as they continued hiking down toward the canyon containing the Little River waterfalls (a series of falls ranging from twenty to forty feet high with sheer canyon walls).

Carly was working on her moss rope late Saturday morning—over two hours after Warden had left—when she thought she heard someone yelling. She stopped her work, and immediately stood up and walked out into the open as far as she could get from the falls on the west bank of the pool. There it was again. Yes. She was certain she heard shouting.

"I'm down here!" she yelled at the top of her lungs. "I'm down here. Help me!"

"Carly!" she heard faintly. Someone was calling *her name*.

"Help me! Please someone help me. I'm down here. God please let them hear me. Please let them find me," she prayed out loud.

"Carly! Carly!" there were several different voices yelling. They knew she was there. Someone must have caught Warden when he went out to get supplies. Thank God, I'm saved. "Thank you, God."

"Carly! Carly!" the voices grew louder and clearer.

"Help!" she screamed, "I'm right down here. Keep going. Help me!" It's Jeff. "Thank God, it's you, Jeff."

"Carly!" Jeff shouted. "Carly!"

"Jeff!" she cried. "Jeff, I'm right here." She noticed that the voices sounded like they were coming from downstream, on the east bank of the canyon. "Jeff, go upstream!" she yelled.

It sounded like the voices were yelling in the opposite direction now.

Then they gradually began to fade.

"No, dear God. Please help them find me," Carly pleaded. "Jeff! I'm up here." She cried and screamed for them. But the voices grew distant, and then they were gone. She crumpled to the bedrock at her feet and wept bitterly. She whispered with her now hoarse voice, "Please God, bring them back."

But there was nothing.

An hour passed and they never came back.

It was Jeff. They were so close.

How did they *not* hear me?

The waterfalls. The noise from the waterfalls must have covered the sound. Oh God, I'll never get out of here alive. It was 1:30. She lay on the bedrock, exhausted, and drifted off to sleep. Her moss pile and moss rope still lay behind the falls where she left it when she first heard the voices.

19

Over the Edge

While the nine team members stood at the edge of the steep cliff overlooking the roaring waterfalls below them to the west, Jeff pointed downstream, and said, "My dad and I camped and fished somewhere down that way. It's not as steep down there. We'll keep yelling for Carly, as we work in that direction."

He led the way downstream along the cliff bluff lined with huckleberry, Oregon grape and salal bushes. Oak, fir and some cedar trees provided the overhead canopy.

"It's amazing how loud those waterfalls are, even on a small stream like this," said Tim. "Yeah, they make it next to impossible to hear much else," Jeff answered.

"We're not gonna find Carly out here you guys," said Kelly. "Can we just go back and drive the roads some more?"

"Yeah, maybe one of the other teams has located that pickup by now," suggested Mandy.

"I just want to go a little farther, around the next bend, so I can show you the spot we camped," Jeff said. "It'll only take another three minutes to reach it."

After Jeff had showed the other eight where he and his dad camped several years earlier, they headed back up the way they had come. The hike out was all uphill.

When they had hiked about half a mile, and were near the highest falls, suddenly Kelly, the fifth person in line, caught her left foot on the base of an Oregon-grape bush and tumbled toward the cliff edge on her right.

She screamed, "No!" as she disappeared over the edge.

The others immediately clung to the closest bushes or trees to them and looked over the steep bank to locate her. When they couldn't see her, and didn't hear a sound from her in the ten seconds or so that passed after her fall, they feared the worst– that when they spotted her, she would be busted up, with blood draining from her mouth, laying on the bedrock bank of the stream below.

"There she is," said Bob. "Right there on that root wad." He pointed to it.

"Kelly, are you alright?" said Jeff.

No answer. No movement.

As luck had it, Kelly landed, belly down, ten feet below the bluff on the root wad of a dead, fallen, twenty-inch-diameter fir tree that was facing downhill at a sixty-degree angle about two feet from the canyon face. Its needle-less crown lay in the middle of the stream below. Many of its branches were broken off, and there were no branches visible within ten feet of Kelly. Its ground support had obviously eroded away years earlier causing its perfectly placed demise.

"Kelly," several of them yelled.

Still no answer.

"We've gotta get down to her," said Tim. "She could've broken her neck in the fall—or pierced her chest with a limb or root. She could bleed to death. See if any of you can see anything on that tree beneath her body, any blood, I mean."

Jeff said, "Bryan, Eric, you guys come with me. We've got to get a couple of young, green fir trees that we can secure together and tie to the base of that fir tree behind Tim." He pointed at it. "I've got my hatchet, hunting knife and some nylon cord. Geez, I wish we would have brought some heavier rope. I wasn't figuring on something like this happening. Did any of the rest of you, by chance, bring a hatchet or some rope in your packs?"

"I've got a hatchet," said Bryan.

"We thought we'd just be driving roads," one of them complained. "Then if we found the brown truck, we'd call everyone together to search for Carly."

"Yeah, I had no idea we were gonna be hiking along steep cliffs."

"We shouldn't have been," said Mandy. "This shouldn't have even happened."

"Well, it did," said Jeff. "Now we have to deal with it. Let's go, Bryan."

Then someone heard Kelly moan. "She's alive."

"Alright. Let's work together. Maybe she's not hurt that bad, after all."

"Ten minutes later, Jeff, Eric, and Bryan returned with two freshly cut fir trees, nearly five inches at the butt, and each about twenty-five feet long. They had already cut the tops and many of the branches off the trees. Jeff positioned the trimmed trees on the ground, side by side with their limb-free side down, then used his hatchet to cut off half the remaining limbs. He left only some of those that stuck out to the sides of the trees, so they could provide more surface area. He finished by tying the poles together in five places.

"Okay," he said. "They're ready. A couple of you guys give me a hand."

He lifted the make-shift ladder, shoved the butts out over the cliff edge above Kelly, and with all three of them holding the trees, they eased the butts down to the root wad. Jeff rammed them securely in between two of the larger extended roots near Kelly's

legs. Then he and Tim grabbed the narrower top half of the ladder above the two boys holding it and bent it down several feet to the earlier indicated fir tree. Bryan then tied the tops to the anchor tree, about six feet up from the ground.

"There," Jeff said. "I'll climb down to her. A couple of you guys hold on to these trees."

By then Kelly seemed to be doing better—fortunately nobody

had spotted any blood earlier—she was talking, but she was afraid to move. She didn't know how bad she was hurt, and she certainly didn't want to fall off the root wad to the deadly bedrock waiting below.

In less than a minute, Jeff was sitting on the root wad next to Kelly.

"How are you doing, girl?" he said. "I'm sorry I got you into this mess. Where does it hurt?"

"Where doesn't it hurt?" said Kelly. "It's my own fault for being such a klutz."

"Do you think anything's broken?"

"I can't tell. My ribs hurt pretty bad."

"You're breathing fine, and there's no blood around your mouth, Kelly. So I don't think you've punctured a lung. You do have a pretty good scratch and knot on your forehead. You must've hit it when you landed."

"Actually, I've got a pretty good headache, now that you mention it," she said. "But other than my chest, I think the only other place that hurts pretty bad is my left forearm."

"Yeah, you've got some blood on it. I can't tell from where I'm at how bad it is, though. Okay, try to pull your knees up to your chest, then I'll help you turn around so you can sit upright between these two roots. Whatever you do, don't look down."

Kelly did what Jeff asked, while he held her steady.

"After she was upright, he said, "How are you feeling now?"

"Now that my weight is off my chest, I can breathe better; I don't think it's that bad."

"Your landing was probably cushioned a little by some of the remaining dirt and moss. It could have been a lot worse," he said, sneaking a look at the bedrock twenty feet below. "It *definitely* could have been a lot worse."

"How are you doing, Kelly," asked Mandy.

"I'm okay."

"How are you going to get her up here, Jeff?" Tim asked.

"I'm going to have her stretch out and wrap her arms around the trees. Then I'm going to wrap my long-sleeve shirt around her back, and one of you guy's shirts around her hips and tie good knots. You guys will then undo the poles at the anchor tree and four of you will pull them and Kelly up, while two of you grab her as soon as you can reach her."

"I'm not doing that!" Kelly protested. "There's no way I'm doing that!"

"If you can come up with any better way, Kelly," said Jeff, "I'm open to it."

"What about having her climb up the limbs?" Tim suggested.

"I thought of that," Jeff answered. "How about that, Kelly?"

"No way I'm doing that either. If I slip, I'm hamburger down there."

"That's what I thought you'd say," said Jeff. "Plus, I don't suppose you have any experience climbing small branches on a nearly vertical tree, do you?"

"No I don't," said Kelly. "I'm not much of a country girl."

"So that leaves my plan. There's no other way."

"I can't do that either," she said.

"You don't have a choice, Kelly."

"At any rate," Bryan interrupted, "I think we should ask God for his protection for her while we get her up here,"

"Go for it, big man." said Tim.

After Bryan prayed, he tossed his long-sleeve shirt down to Jeff.

With no other choice, Kelly carefully stretched out while holding onto the two fir trees. Jeff then wrapped and tied her. When she was tied tight, the team on the bluff untied the anchor cord and made ready to haul back.

"Okay," said Jeff. "Haul her up on three."

"One. Two. Three!"

In one steady pull, Kelly was back on the bluff.

"See how easy that was, Kelly," said Tim. "No problem for men like us."

"I'm sure Bryan's prayer didn't hurt either," said Mandy. "Now how are you gonna get up here, Jeff?"

"I'm gonna climb. After you get Kelly untied, you guys position the trees back down to the rootwad the same way we had them before."

After Kelly was released from the poles, the boys shoved them back over the edge. Jeff helped ram them into place on the bottom of the root wad. He then tied them off to a couple of the bigger roots.

"Okay, tie the tops to the tree," Jeff said.

A minute later, "They're tied," said Tim.

"Hold on to the trees now."

The boys grabbed the trees firmly, then said, "We've got them."

Jeff then carefully climbed up the make-shift ladder.

"I'm glad it was you and not me," one of the boys said.

"It was no different than climbing any other tree," said Jeff. "As long as you only move one hand or foot at a time, you have the other three to brace you. Even if one limb broke, you're okay. The other thing is you never look down. You can't even let yourself consider what would happen if you fell, or you might get too nervous and do something dumb."

Mandy finished applying bandages to Kelly's cuts, while Kelly swallowed three Ibuprofen tablets and drank from a canteen. Then, moving at a slow pace for Kelly's sake, the teams hiked out to their three vehicles without further incident.

At 3:45 pm, after driving several miles down Little River Road, Jeff was finally able to make contact with Sam, who reported that none of the other teams had any luck locating a brown pickup. All of the teams besides Jeff's drove roads for another hour then called it quits. Jeff took Kelly to the Roseburg Clinic where she was examined and released with no broken bones, but advised to have her parents watch for signs of concussion during the night.

Back at Safeway for debrief, 6:30 pm, Saturday—

Sam reported what he'd learned from Jeff regarding Kelly's condition, and let Tim tell the others about her misadventure. Then Sam wrapped it up.

"Now that Jeff's not here," said Sam, "I'll say, I think we've done all we can do to find Carly. We're gonna have to leave it in the law's hands now. The reality is, with every passing day, the chances of her being found alive grow slimmer. It's definitely not looking too good." A couple girls broke into tears. "Obviously she can use our prayers. Thanks for all your help. I'll see you all at school, Monday."

20

Where's Warden

When Carly awakened, it was nearly dark. It was not a dream. She was still there. Still trapped in the canyon by the falls.

Alone.

No Jeff.

No friends.

No family.

Hopeless.

It started to rain.

She suddenly remembered she had left the moss and the rope-in-progress lying out in the open. Had he returned? Had he found what she was working on? Where was he? If he *had* returned, why hadn't he wakened her? Was it a trick? Was he watching her all the time, waiting for her to make her big escape, only to catch her at the last minute.

She hurried over to her materials and stashed them in the damp hiding place.

He's never been gone this long. Maybe they did catch him.

100

Maybe they do have a good idea where I am. They have to. They never would have known to look here if they didn't. Maybe they *will* come back looking for me.

The sprinkle broke into an old-fashioned, western Oregon downpour—a cold downpour. She went inside.

They'll be back.

They've got to be back.

They'll be back with airplanes and helicopters.

With a mountainside full of search and rescue people.

After the rain.   During daylight. They'll be back. They'll find me.

Her stomach growled. She was starving. She scraped together some leftover bread and other food and ate her fill. She finished the milk. She grew sleepy. She was too worn-out and stressed to read tonight. She went to the bathroom, changed clothes, then climbed into the sleeping bag.

Like Goldilocks, she fell fast asleep.

But it wasn't the three bears that woke her.

She jerked up from the cot. Something jumped high in the air and landed on her.

The cat.

"Happy. Oh, Happy, I'm so glad to see you."

"*I'm not alone.* I have you. We came so close to being rescued today," she said, as she stroked his favorite spots, and listened to him purr so soothingly.

"You're the best cat in the world. We're gonna get out of here. You just wait and see. I'll take you with me, or at least come back for you. Are you hungry? You're definitely not skinny. I bet you find all the food you want out here, don't you, boy. My step dad always said cats were the most adaptable animal known to man. I think he was right. He was right about a lot of things.

"But now he's in jail, and he didn't even do anything wrong. Just like my mom's restraining order against him. He never hurt a flea, or even threatened to. God, take care of him in jail tonight. Let them find out that he's innocent.

"Maybe they already know he's innocent. That's right. If they caught Warden today, they know Ken's innocent. They probably released him already. I bet he's gonna come for me. Please God, *let him* come for me."

She lay back down, and Happy snuggled up to her neck and head. His purring put her to sleep in no time.

She dreamed of Christmas when she was seven. It was the second one with her new stepfather, Ken, and his two teenage boys. They were at Grandma and Grandpas' place. Everyone was there, at least everyone on her mom's side of the family. Her two brothers and sister, Grandma, Grandpa, her Aunt Maggie, her uncles, all of their families.

Strings of various colored lights flickered on and off on the tree and on the strands hung around the house. They opened the mountain of fancily-wrapped presents encircling the beautifully decorated tree. The dinner with turkey and all the trimmings was out of this world. The women in the family could really cook. Everyone was having a great time.

Then it happened. Grandma opened her big mouth. The room suddenly went quiet, as tension hung heavy. They had all been there before. When Grandma was around, a great time could go sour in a hurry. Everyone always hoped they'd get through without her saying something insensitive or rude to someone. But it didn't happen this time.

Grandma said those horrible things to Ken. Why did she always have to find fault with him? And in front of the whole family, no less.

Carly awakened from her dream before the crisis played out. But she remembered it. Her poor ex-stepfather: always the subject of Grandma's attacks. Carly wondered why Grandma had it in for him. It never made sense to her. And then everyone always made excuses for her afterward. "You know Grandma, she can't help herself. It's just the way she is." Like that made it okay.

Ken never went to another family holiday after that. Who could blame him? He'd been humiliated one too many times.

Carly finally managed to fall back to sleep, with Happy at her side.

Sunday morning, Five days missing—

She woke to the smell of French toast and syrup. She opened her eyes. He was back. She was relieved. Then she was sad, realizing what that meant. He hadn't been caught. That meant *they* probably *didn't know* she was there.

But why had Jeff and the others come for me?

Maybe they hadn't.

Maybe it was all a dream.

Maybe I'm losing it.

Maybe I want them to come so much that I imagined it.

Hearing their voices.

But it was so real.

If it was them, why couldn't they hear me when I yelled? That's what happens in dreams; things just don't work quite right. If I could hear them, they should've been able to hear me. And why was it Jeff and not the police or search and rescue people? He couldn't possibly know where I am, especially since I'm hours away from Roseburg. And if he did know, he would've had the police with him. Maybe he did. If he did, they would have found me. They wouldn't have given up until they *did* find me. It wasn't real.

I'm never getting out of here.

He's got me, and I'm never going home.

She turned over to face away from him. Happy was gone.

She cried silently.

21

Grandma's Girl

"**Carly**, I've made you some French toast this morning," Warden said.

"I don't want any. I'm gonna stay in bed all day."

"Is that what you tell your mom on Sunday: the Lord's day?"

"What would you know about the Lord's day? Nobody that takes girls could possibly know anything about that. Or care."

"I guess when you're as popular as you are, you have everything figured out, including me," he said.

"There's nothing to figure out. You took me to try to replace your daughters. But it's never gonna happen. You're not my dad, and I'm not your daughter."

"It's funny. Just when I think I've made some progress with you, you go back to being the defiant, stubborn, mouthy Carly. How long's it going to take?"

"How long's it gonna take?" she mimicked him. "That's what I'd like to know. How long's it gonna take for you to let me go home?"

"How long it takes is partly up to you, Carly."

"Don't start playing your head games with me. If you planned to ever let me go, you wouldn't have kept me here this long already. You made me miss my team's most important game of the year Friday night. They probably got stomped without me."

"Would that make you happy, if your team *did* get stomped without you? Would that make you feel more important?"

"You're so cruel."

"No. I'm not cruel," he said. "What I'm saying to you isn't cruel. It's a gift."

"Right," she said. "So now you think you're a gift to me because you play your little mind games."

"For your information, your team won its game by one point. Kristin checked a Sheldon girl's lay up with time running out."

Carly jerked up and swung her legs off the cot, placed her feet on the floor and faced him. "They won? They beat Sheldon without me?"

"Hard to believe, isn't it, Carly?—that your team, without you, could beat a top team like Sheldon, on its home floor where it hadn't lost in two seasons."

"They actually won? Or are you just saying that? How would you know anyway? Did you hear it on your truck radio?"

"Yes, they actually won. It doesn't matter how I found out. What matters is what you learn from it?"

"Here you go again. Who died and made you my counselor anyway?"

"You know what's amazing to me, Carly?"

"What?"

"That you can talk to anyone like that, let alone the person that has complete control over your life and your future right now."

"You mean *whether* I have a future, don't you?"

"If that's the case, that I have power over whether you have a future, how can you be so arrogant to talk to me so disrespectfully? Is that how you talked to your stepfather?"

"I figured you'd bring it around to him sooner or later. Do you have a *fetish* about him?"

"Haven't you learned anything in church over the years, Carly? Using words like foreplay and fetish. So unladylike, don't you think?"

"You're one to talk. Is taking me and keeping me against my wishes, being a gentleman? Hardly. And who are you to bring up the Lord's Day or church? Give me a break."

"I can see I'm not going to get anywhere with you this morning," he said, getting up. "I'm going to leave you to yourself for while. Maybe when I come back you'll act more like a lady."

"Suit yourself."

He left her to her breakfast and went out to who knows where.

After he was gone, she thought, *Can't you ever keep your trap shut, Carly?* You're sounding just like Grandma. If you want to get out of here alive, you better somehow keep your mouth shut, and at least play along. Tell him what he wants to hear. You're good at that. You know how to say what you have to in order to get your way. Now would be the perfect time to do that.

Lunch at Grandma and Grandpa Windbags' house in Roseburg, after church—

"Mom, I don't know what I'm going to do if they don't find Carly alive," said Glenda, Carly's mom,

"We've got to trust the Lord, honey" answered Carly's Grandma. "It's in his hands now. Surely he won't let any harm come to her. *Not a good girl like her.*" Like *any* girl deserved to be harmed. Who would she have to criticize and brag about so much if Carly didn't come back?

"I know Ken had to have taken her," said Glenda, "no matter what the police think. He was gone for those days and had no alibi."

"He's guilty as sin, and we all know it," said Grandma. "Who else would have a reason to take her? Everyone loves her. And everyone knows how important she is to this community and high school. He was always jealous that she was so much more talented than his own worthless kids. He's the only one that could possibly have taken her."

"Just because you never liked Ken, doesn't mean you have to criticize his boys so much, Mom."

"I thought you stopped making excuses for them a few years ago, honey. Why would you stick up for them now? They're not part of this family anymore. We don't have to pretend to like them any longer."

Carly's grandpa wanted to tell her to put a lid on it, but as always didn't dare. Not unless he wanted to get an earful of her condemnation, and have to sleep on the couch for the next week. He learned years ago not to go against her tide. She had verbally drowned him plenty of times in the early years of their marriage. *She wore the pants*. He knew it. She knew it. Everyone in the family knew it. And sadly, everyone that had ever spent anytime around them knew it. He was quite a man. And she was quite a woman—quite a hypocritical woman.

22

More News Clippings

Back in the shack, Sunday afternoon—

"What are you reading, Carly?" asked Warden, when he came in and saw her lying on the cot with a book open.

"It's *The Angel of Marin Island*."

"Do you like to read about angels?"

"I never have before, but it's not like I have a lot to pick from here. I've already read two books through. Just thought I'd try this one for a change of pace."

"How is it?"

"Pretty interesting. It's about how an angel helps a teenage boy and girl that get stranded on an island when their boat is damaged on the rocky shoreline. Haven't you read all the books here?"

"Actually, I haven't," he said. "They're suited more for your age-group. Not that I wouldn't find any of them interesting. They're just not the type of books I normally read."

"Oh."

"Do you believe in angels, Carly?"

"Yes, but I don't really know much about them. They're God's messengers, His helpers. That's about all I know. Do you believe in them, Warden?"

He was surprised to hear her grant him the respect of using his name. She must have had a change of heart since this morning.

"I believe in them, but probably not in the way you do."

"Yeah," she said, "I guess you couldn't believe in them much, or God either, to be doing what you've done with me."

He acted like he didn't hear her comment, sat down at the table and said nothing for several seconds. Then he asked, "Did you ever read or hear of the passage in the Bible that says something about not neglecting to show hospitality to strangers because the strangers some people have entertained were angels and they didn't even know it?"

"Yeah, I've heard that before."

"That passage, of course, would naturally imply that any stranger that any of us meet could actually be an angel. And if that's actually true, don't you think it should affect the way we treat strangers?"

"Yeah, Warden, I'm actually an angel: *you have kidnapped an angel*," she said sarcastically. "Where does that leave you? I'd say headed straight for you-know-where."

"I'm sure you're not an angel, Carly," he said. "So what about you? Do you treat strangers, or more accurately, strange kids—those at least who you, miss popular, all-world, Carly Cantwell, think are strange—the way you would if you knew they were actually angels sent by God?"

"Who does? Why are you pushing me so hard? I'm no worse than anyone else in the way I treat people. Heck, the Bible says a ton about loving our neighbors and even our enemies, but who really does that either?"

"You've got a good point there, Carly. But that doesn't clear you of your own personal responsibility to treat other people with kindness, does it?"

"Like I should listen to you, the kidnapper," she said. "I think you better change the subject to something that doesn't step on your own toes."

He reached into his jacket and pulled out some more newspaper, separated a couple pages, then said, "I wanted to show you another newspaper clipping about that accident."

"Oh yeah, I forgot all about that," she answered.

He handed a page to her and said, "Here, read it out loud for me."

"Why do you always want me to read these things out loud?"

"It makes them seem more like news reports that way."

"Yeah, now that you mention it, I think it does," she said.

Dated September 20, 1998
Star Quarterback Upgraded
Search Called Off for Missing Driver

Astoria High School star quarterback Bryan Russell's condition was upgraded to fair by Columbia Memorial Hospital staff yesterday.

Russell was seriously injured early Saturday morning, September 16th in the fiery roll-over car accident on Astoria-Megler Bridge that claimed the life of his sixteen-year-old girlfriend Susan Hope Fitzgerald. The driver of the other vehicle, Edward Don Bradley, 36, is still missing. According to Russell, Bradley—who was on fire—jumped the 200 feet from the bridge into the Columbia River. Russell said it was the last thing he saw before he passed out.

U.S. Coast Guard officials said they called off the search for Bradley at dark yesterday.

The Clatsop County Sheriff's Department said that neither Russell or Fitzgerald were wearing seat belts and both were well over the adult legal alcohol limit for drivers at the time of the accident. The department said they found no evidence in Bradley's burned vehicle of open alcohol containers and none of

the local drinking establishments had seen him earlier in the evening. The investigation into the accident is continuing.

Carly handed the clipping back to Warden and said, "So your daughter was killed because her boyfriend drove drunk? That must have caused you even more pain when you found that out."

"Yes. Why she was drinking that night is anyone's guess. I heard that everyone who knew her said she never drank more than a beer or two any other time."

"Were any charges filed against her boyfriend over it?"

"Here, read about it for yourself." He handed her another clipping.

Dated November 21, 1998

Astoria Quarterback Charged
With Manslaughter

Clatsop County District Attorney Pete Bonaventure filed manslaughter charges against Astoria High School star quarterback Bryan Russell yesterday in the death of his girlfriend, Susan Hope Fitzgerald, and the presumed death of Edward Don Bradley.

Fitzgerald was killed on the Astoria-Megler Bridge in the wee hours Saturday morning, September 16th, when she was ejected, then crushed by the car driven by Russell, who was found to be legally drunk at the time of the accident. Bradley, the driver of the pickup hit by Russell's car, has been missing since he jumped off the 200-foot-bridge, while on fire, into the Columbia River. Coast Guard and local law enforcement officials called off the search for Bradley on September 19th.

When Astoria High School varsity head football coach Frank Milton was asked about his feelings regarding the charges against his side-lined quarterback, he wouldn't comment.

Clatsop County Sheriff spokesman Rawl Terwilliger said,

"Our department does not wish to give a statement regarding the charges, other than to acknowledge that alcohol definitely played a huge factor in the tragic accident." He also admitted there were major discrepancies between Russell's account of the accident and the Sheriff and Oregon State Police Departments' findings.

According to Terwilliger the police investigation determined that Russell had been passing Bradley but cut back in front of him too soon. The right rear of his Chevelle collided with the left front of Bradley's Ford pickup, causing Bradley's vehicle to veer to the right and career off the right side of the bridge, before coming back across the highway and smashing into the left side of the bridge, where it exploded into flames. Upon hitting Bradley's pickup, Russell's car rolled over multiple times ejecting Fitzgerald, then rolling over her.

Neither the Russell family or its attorney would comment on the charges.

"So was the Russell kid convicted?" asked Carly.

"Yes, though the case never went to trial. After learning that he would be tried as an adult—despite his being a month shy of eighteen at the time of the accident—and that the state was going for two counts of first degree manslaughter and a ten year minimum sentence, Russell and his attorney accepted a plea-agreement in which he admitted that the state's findings regarding the accident were correct. He was ultimately charged with two counts of Third Degree Involuntary Manslaughter. He was sentenced to five years in the Oregon State Prison, but was paroled after three years."

"The price some kids have to pay to learn a lesson," said Carly. "Drinking and driving don't mix. He has to live with what he did for the rest of his life."

"The interesting thing is," said Warden, "Susan's mother and adoptive father forgave the Russell boy for their daughter's death publicly, in the courtroom before he was sentenced, saying that their prayer was that the young people of the community would learn from the accident and never drink and drive."

"Like kids ever learn from other kids' mistakes," she said. "Oh they might tow-the-line for a short time after a kid gets seriously injured or killed. But then they go back to doing the same dangerous things they did before, figuring what happened to the other kid won't happen to them. What about you, Warden, were you ever able to forgive him? How did you deal with her death?"

"That's something I'd rather not talk about now," he said, surprising her.

23

Stepfather Known

They both sat for a few minutes without speaking, then Carly said, "Will you take your mask off for me, Warden?"

"Why is that important to you, Carly? It doesn't matter what I look like."

"You don't know what it's like spending days with a man, talking with him, and never getting to see his face."

"Maybe *everyone* should wear masks, so pretty girls like you, who have so much going for them, wouldn't judge them by their outward looks. Do you think it is fair the way people are judged by their outward appearance? Kids are real bad about it. All the prettiest girls seem to get all the positive attention, especially from the boys, while the plain-looking ones, or the less fortunate, unattractive, ugly or fat girls either get little attention or negative attention. Of course, those like yourself, who have always gotten the positive attention, don't know what it's like to be those *other* kids."

She said, "Sometimes I get the feeling that besides wanting me to replace your daughters, you have me here to point out all my faults, to make me pay for being who I am, and to try to change me into being something I'm not. Then, of course, there's your little hang up with my ex-stepfather. What is it with your interest in the way things were with him anyway?"

"What if I told you I know your stepfather?"

"You know him? *You know* my stepfather?" she said, with obvious hope in her voice.

"I haven't seen him in quite a while, but yes I know him pretty well," he said.

"So did he tell you all about me, and all the problems he had in his marriage to my mom, all the in-law problems, all of it?"

"He told me enough about you and the issues with his marriage to your mom, for me to get a feel for what he was dealing with."

"Why have you listened to me say the things I have, and didn't tell me you know him?"

"I've found that often the best approach to learning about someone is to just listen to them without telling them everything you know. You can get to know a lot about what's important to someone by listening.

"So now that the cat's out of the bag, tell me why *if* you know my stepfather, you kidnapped me. Does it have anything to do with him?"

"Actually it has to do with you. I thought you were figuring that out," he said.

"I don't believe that. You've been *too* interested in my stepfather for it to just have to do with me."

"You're right, Carly. It has to do with you *and* him, and also helping you to look hard at the person you've become as opposed to the person you should be."

"Oh, here you go with the psychoanalysis crap again. Would you give up on that already?"

"Call it what you want. But you're here, I'm here, we're both going to be here until we get the things accomplished that we need to," he said.

"What gives with you? If I didn't know better I'd think my stepfather hired you to do all this to me. Is he so desperate for a relationship with me that he'd pay money to have me kidnapped and brainwashed to get me to come back to him, or whatever it is he wants?"

"You can't help yourself, can you, Carly? Your self-importance shows itself in so many ways. But you know what I think?"

"I don't really care what you think, Warden. *What do you think?*"

"And females wonder why guys can't understand them," he answered. "What I think is that so much of what you say and do to show your confidence, to make others believe you are so great, is just a cover up for how inadequate you really feel inside."

"You said a mouthful there, didn't you?"

"You can't deny the truth in what I said though, can you?"

She sat silently for half a minute. Again, he was right.

"What did my stepfather say anyway?" she asked, moving right along.

"I'll tell you more about that later," he answered. "Right now, I'm going to go for a hike in the woods."

Part of Carly wanted him to just go jump off a cliff, so she could be done with him and escape. But the other part of her was curious about what his connection was to her ex-stepfather, and what he'd been told about her. In the last four days, she'd been stirred inside with feelings for her stepfather that she didn't know she had— feelings that lay dormant deep inside her. Feelings that her mom, grandma, and other family members didn't know still existed. Feelings they had all worked hard to extinguish.

While Warden was gone, Carly went outside, under the falls, and worked feverishly braiding strands of moss together. After an hour, she stretched out what she had completed so far to see how long it was. Near as she could tell, it was about twenty feet. She was almost halfway there, allowing for the length she would need to tie it off.

In her abundant spare time, she had done a lot of thinking about what would be the best way to escape. She could go up, by using a rock or waterlogged stick to heave her moss rope up. The problem with trying to go up was that it would be difficult to heave her rope high enough to reach the top of the cliffs around the pool. Then, even if she could get it that high, she'd never be able to fasten it securely.

Her only viable option was to go down. She would tie the upper end of her rope off to a strong, well-anchored root on the cliff wall beside the pool, or around the base of one of the big boulders, throw the other end off the cliff to the ledge below and shinny down the rope. Of course, she would have to test the rope on a short climb before actually making her escape to ensure it had the strength to hold her.

She continued working on the moss rope for another hour. By then it was getting dark. She coiled the growing rope up, dunked it in the pool for several seconds, then stuffed it and the unused stringy moss back inside her secret damp crevice. Then she laid some wet green moss across the opening.

She felt if all went well, that if Warden left her alone during daylight for most of another day, she would have enough rope to make her escape. Then she would go the day after that when she'd have most of a day to hike.

Just as she headed inside, she heard Warden's cable ladder land against the base of the cliff beside the pool. She went in and quickly wiped her arms off so he wouldn't figure out what she'd been doing in his absence. With the weather improving, she would wash clothes in the pool first thing in the morning.

24

The Windbag

Monday morning, 6 days missing—

Warden made Carly some Cream of Wheat, and gave her some grapes and milk, for breakfast, then left before she was done eating. He said he would be gone most the day.

She wondered why he gave that away. Was he really going to be gone that long, or was this a setup so he could catch her trying to escape? And if he actually was going to be gone for so long, where was he going? She was very afraid that sooner or later he'd catch on to what she was doing with the moss and spoil the whole escape effort. She had to get away soon, before it was too late.

At the Douglas County jail—

Carly's ex-stepfather, Ken Roderick, was released at 10 am. His attorney threatened to sue the district attorney's office for holding him without sufficient evidence and basing its entire case against him on *three things* which wouldn't hold weight in the courtroom: First, his ex-wife (Carly's mom) and ex-in-laws' accusations of his

119

involvement in Carly's abduction. Second, the fact that he had no alibi at the time she went missing and for the days immediately following. And third, Carly's two hairs that were found in a sleeping bag that was unrolled in Roderick's pickup bed at the time of his arrest. Carly's mom admitted Carly had slept in that bag numerous times before the marriage broke up.

Over at the sheriff's office, Sheriff Wolvord told Detective Hampton that the FBI would keep a discreet surveillance on Roderick. Unlike Hampton, the FBI believed Roderick was still a good suspect in his ex-stepdaughter's disappearance. Hampton wasn't buying that. He felt confident that Roderick was being honest with him on every point. And he also couldn't see where Roderick had any motive for kidnapping her, regardless of what his ex-wife and ex-in-laws said about him.

At Roseburg High School, students talking at lunch—

"Carly's step dad was released today. What's up with that?"

"Maybe they figure he'll lead them to her."

"Let's hope so."

"Did you see the state polls this morning?"

"No."

"Our girls' basketball team has moved up to second."

"They obviously don't know the key player is gone indefinitely—maybe even dead."

"Maybe they do, and the win Friday over Sheldon just proved how good they are, even without her."

"Are the boys rated?"

"Yes. They're at number ten."

"They made it to number eight or so three years ago, then lost their last five games, including their league playoff game."

"The boys' basketball program hasn't had near the success that the football and wrestling teams have."

"I heard Sam's ranked first in state in his weight class now."

"He's got to be one of the toughest kids in school."

"And one of the most handsome."

"Kaylin said he's planning to go into the marines as soon as school's out."

"Let's hope not. He could end up in Iraq or Afghanistan."

"His dad's ex-marine. A two-tour Vietnam vet."

"No wonder he's so tough."

"My cousin's dad was killed in Vietnam when he was only three."

"That must have been rough, growing up without a dad."

"His mom remarried a couple years later, so he had a dad—just not his."

Detective Hampton on the phone with Carly's grandma, who called him—

"Look, Mrs. Windbag," said Hampton, "our department, the state police, the Roseburg police, and the FBI are all doing all we can to find your granddaughter."

"Well it's obviously not enough," the grandma said. "You're sitting in your office, on your duff, while my Carly is out there with some monster."

"I thought you were convinced that your ex-son-in-law took her?"

"What did you let that piece-of-scum go for, anyway?"

"He told me you were a Christian woman. You aren't sounding much like one now."

"He told you that? What else did he tell you?"

"I'm sorry, Mrs. Windbag, I can't get into that with you. But I'm convinced he isn't involved in your granddaughter's abduction."

"So you just let him prance out of your station like he owned the place, I bet."

"Not that it matters to me, Mrs. Windbag, but why do you have it in so much for Roderick anyway? He strikes me as a very decent individual, with no police record, other than the restraining order your daughter placed on him."

"He's just never been caught before. The man's a controller."

"I've got to cut this off in a minute, so I can get off my duff and look for your granddaughter. But I'm curious, what did he do to make you believe he's a controller?"

"I used to be able to stop by my daughter's place, without having the decency or consideration of calling first, and take Carly with me anytime I wanted with no regard for the plans the family might have. But soon after *he* married my daughter, he observed how I always put her in a no-win situation and called me on it. Also, I didn't like it when I was at their house and he tried to stop me from involving myself in his and my daughter's conversations, dealing with various family matters, which were none of my business."

"Sounds like he was just being a normal husband and father, and you were the one who was out of line," said Hampton.

"Wouldn't you know it? The guy investigating Carly's disappearance is in cahoots with my daughter's ex-husband." She wasn't about to refer to him as her ex-son-in-law.

"I've got to go now, Mrs. Windbag. We'll definitely get a hold of you when we find out anything, or just feel like listening to you *break wind.*"

All morning, Carly took advantage of Warden's absence working diligently braiding more string moss into her rope. By noon, she had added seven feet of length. But her fingers and hands grew tired. She had reached her limit for the day.

She carefully stashed things, then went inside, fixed and ate a sandwich, then relaxed on the cot for a while. Happy came in and kept her company.

At shortly before 1:30, she went back out to soak up a little sun before it fell behind the firs to the southwest at around 2:30. She didn't know when Warden would be back, and definitely wasn't looking forward to the psycho session she anticipated upon his return. What was he trying to prove anyway?

25

Step Father Memories

At a little before 4 pm, Carly saw the cable ladder flop down across the creek from her. He was back. She tensed up. She didn't know why. Maybe it was because she felt locked into the same daily routine, like a ritual. The masked man—like the lone ranger—kept coming back to rescue her from her boredom, from her loneliness, from her sense of hopelessness, from her prison. But then, each time, she discovered *he's not here to rescue me*.

He's here to keep me—to keep me here in *his* prison, far away from everything important to me.

When he reached the bottom of the ladder, he turned around, and said loudly, to be heard over the crashing water, "Did you have a good day, Carly?"

"You aren't serious, are you?" she said. "You don't have any idea what it's like to spend my whole day here with nothing to do but read, sleep, and maybe toss rocks into the pool."

He walked along the right side of the long pool, and said to Carly, who was standing on the opposite side, "Don't you spend some of your time thinking?"

"Of course. I do plenty of thinking. More than I want. But I'm an active teen. I'm getting out of shape just sitting around here. When I get out of here, I'll be so out of shape my teammates will run circles around me."

"What day is today, Carly?"

"Monday."

"So you've gone five days without doing anything physical and you think you're out of shape?"

"You must not have done any sports if you don't know that," she said.

"I already told you I coached softball."

"You don't have to be in great shape to play softball. It's nothing like running up and down the basketball court. We run lines every-day at the end of practice to help us stay in shape. I'm sure not doing that here."

"If you wanted, you could do plenty here to stay in shape: such as various calisthenics and running in place or even around this shelf. But trust me, as good of shape as you were in, you haven't lost enough in five days to make any big difference."

"By saying that, are you telling me that you're going to let me go soon?"

"That's not what I meant. We still haven't accomplished enough."

"Well then, can we just get to it?"

Warden sat down on his favorite boulder near the pool, and waited for Carly to walk clear around the stream to take a seat on the one next to him. She noticed that he hadn't put the ladder away, and suddenly got the idea that if she could pick up a good size rock and hit him on the head; this was her chance to escape. As he seemed preoccupied with staring at the water in the pool, she walked slowly around from the far side of the falls and crossed in behind his boulder which was fifty feet downstream from the falls.

There, directly back of him, just to her right, was the perfect size rock, oval shaped, about ten inches long by about five inches around. She took a step toward it and started to bend down to grab it.

"Are you going to come sit down?" he asked, without turning around.

She startled. It was no use. She could never go through with it anyway. She stood, then moved over to her boulder, to the right of his, and sat on it.

"Tell me about the two most fun things you ever did with your step dad," he said.

She thought: I know what he's up to. Now he's going to start calling him my stepdad instead of stepfather, and he's going to try to get me to focus on the things I liked about him. He's *so* predictable, just like the school counselor. They must've received their psychology degrees from the same school. Or maybe that's just the way all counselors are. They try to manipulate you into reaching the outcome that *they* think is best for you. I hate manipulators.

"I'll give you a minute to remember, okay."

She didn't answer. He sat quietly, waiting while she thought.

Finally, "Well one time we were camped at Wickiup Reservoir in the Cascade Mountains. I think I was about ten. It was just him, me and my mom. By then his boys were in their late teens and didn't go camping with us as much."

"Anyway, he was catching a bunch of catfish during the day in his twelve foot john boat. From our camp near the lake, I saw all the action he was having and so I grabbed my fishing pole and ran down to the sandy beach near where he was anchored. He got a huge smile on his face when I got near the water. I started laughing. Then he started laughing. He knew I wanted to get in on all the action. He immediately pulled up his anchor and rowed over to pick me up."

"For two hours, we caught one catfish after another. I had the time of my life." At first Carly smiled as she told the story, but then the smile turned to a sad face. A tear drained from her right eye, down her cheek. She remembered. He had taken her fishing many times. And she'd always had fun.

Warden let the emotions of her memory play out. Then, after a few minutes of silence, asked, "Can you tell me about another fun time with him, Carly?"

A minute passed. She didn't want to recall the good times. It was too painful.

"Carly?"

Another minute. He wasn't putting too much pressure on her. She appreciated that.

"Yeah, I remember another thing. It wasn't really something fun that he and I did together. It was just something that used to mean a lot to me; used to make me feel so happy. So loved. So safe. And so much a part of a family."

"What's that, Carly? Go ahead," he said, knowing he was making progress now.

"About six months after he married my mom, we were all playing ball in the backyard with a beach ball. Mom, Dad, me and his boys." She had obviously lost herself in the memory. "Just hitting the ball around in the air. At one point, all four of them collided and fell to the ground. No one was hurt, but they were all lying in a pile, laughing. I was standing a few feet away and suddenly got an idea. I piled on to them and wrapped my arms around them as much as my little arms would reach and said, 'Family hug.'"

"They all laughed at me as we hugged in one huge hug, and everyone said, 'family hug.'" Carly started crying. "From then on— at least until the big Christmas blowup over a year later—whenever I saw the opportunity, I initiated the family hug. I wanted so much to be part of a family that loved each other. I felt so safe and loved when we did our family hugs. I loved to see Mom and Dad hug each other. I wanted them to love each other with all their hearts."

"But I thought you said you quit calling your stepdad *dad* after the first argument your grandma caused between him and your mom."

"I did, most the time, at least."

"What did you call him?"

"At first I called him Ken. But he didn't like that so he, Mom and I agreed that I would call him Pappy."

"So is that what you called him, Pappy?"

"Sometimes. But after awhile I didn't call him anything."

"Why did you do that?"

"I knew he didn't like it. It gave me a sort of power over him. And I knew that Grandma and others in the family didn't want me to. They didn't want me to call him Dad or Pappy."

"But he *was* your dad. He was your pappy."

"Not according to my grandma, Aunt Maggie and my older brothers."

"So they cheated you out of being able to call Ken, 'Dad?'" he said.

She didn't answer. She choked up.

"You said that you didn't call him Dad much after that. So when *did you* call him Dad?"

He already knew the answer. It wouldn't take a rocket scientist to figure it out.

"Carly?"

Nothing.

"I bet you called him Dad when you wanted something from him, didn't you. When you wanted to manipulate him?"

Nothing.

They both knew he was right, but he wanted her to admit it.

Finally, he said, "I'm right aren't I, Carly? You only addressed him, "Dad," when you really wanted your way. You knew he'd give in to that every time, didn't you?"

"Yes." She burst into tears. "I said Dad, when I really needed to get my way. I manipulated him. Are you satisfied? I'm a *manipulator* too, on top of all my other faults." She hated manipulators. She hated herself for being one.

"This is good, Carly. We're really getting somewhere now."

She was broken. This time she didn't even think of making a smart comment about how cruel he was. He was right. But she hated him for forcing her to face herself. She didn't know how much more of this she could take. This isn't fair, God. You let this monster kidnap me for this. Please make it all end. I just want to go back to my regular life.

"We're getting much closer, Carly. I don't think it will be long now."

What's that mean, she wondered, *it may not be long now*? Until you let me go? Until you've satisfied yourself? Until you've made me into the perfect little girl your Susan was?

He knew she'd had enough for the evening. He let her go inside, then followed her. He pulled a roll of summer sausage, some cheese and crackers out of his pack and set them on the table, along with a knife. She saw the knife, but was too worn out emotionally to even consider how she could get it. He cut off some beef sausage and cheese and put together a bunch of cracker sandwiches. He then pulled out the bottle of orange juice from his pack and poured them each a cup.

After they had eaten, he said he was leaving for the night: that he would be out in the woods nearby. He'd be back in the morning.

He left.

She went to the bathroom, then came out and crashed on her bed. She was sound asleep in no time. Happy came in and lay beside her, but she didn't notice. It had been a tough day.

26

Warden's Discovery

The next morning, Tuesday, one week missing—

Warden made Carly some eggs and toast for breakfast. After she had eaten, he said, "Carly, I found something in the woods downstream from here this morning that concerns me."

"What'd you find?"

"I found evidence that someone was up here two or three days ago."

"Someone was up here?" she acted surprised. They *were here* then. It wasn't a dream, or my imagination.

"I found a couple of young fir trees tied together with cord. Someone had used them for a ladder of sorts. But I'm puzzled about why they used it where they did."

"Where was that?" she asked.

"About a hundred-fifty yards downstream."

"They used a ladder that close to here? What's that mean?"

"I don't know. Maybe they were out here looking for you. I found blood there too."

"Blood?"

"Yes. The ladder was used to get down to an upturned tree over the edge of the cliff. There was some blood on one of the tree's roots."

She wasn't about to tell him she heard Jeff and some other people yelling for her on Saturday. If he knew that, he would move her away from here to someplace where no one would ever find her.

"What do you think happened?" she asked.

"My best guess is that one of the people must have slipped over the edge of the bluff and luckily landed on the root wad of the fallen tree. If they hadn't, they would have been killed landing on the bedrock at the bottom."

She wondered if the person was hurt bad, and whether it could have been Jeff or one of her other classmates that fell.

"I'm thinking we might have to move from here," he said.

"They're not going to find me down here. And whoever it was was probably just out for a weekend hike or something. If they had been looking for me, don't you think they would have found me? And why would they even look *here* for me?"

"I don't know the answers to your questions. But I'm concerned. Maybe someone spotted my truck."

"It couldn't have been that," she said. "And if they had, how would they connect it to me? They wouldn't." She hoped desperately that they had, in fact, seen his truck and knew there was a connection to her.

"You're probably right, Carly. It was probably just some kids out for a hike. It's just very rare anyone comes near here. That's one of the reasons I like it here."

"I'm sure they won't come back. I couldn't get that lucky."

"I wouldn't say that," he said. "You said yourself you get a lot of breaks."

"I didn't get a break when you kidnapped me, did I?"

"Actually, you did. And someday you'll understand that."

Changing the subject, Carly said, "My team's playing South

Eugene tonight. They're the only team we've lost to. And we never should have lost that game. They're no where near as good as we are."

"It sounds like your team must have been overconfident."

"Yeah, we were. Coach Hollister even warned us during practice the night before. He said we weren't working hard enough, that we thought we could beat South Eugene with our eyes closed."

"He's a good coach. When I used to coach I told the girls that you can't ever overlook any opponent, because when you do, that's when you'll get beat. I bet your team won't take them lightly this time."

"I'm sure they won't either. Please, Warden, can you take me back home now. I don't want to miss anymore games."

"They couldn't let you play tonight even if you did go home, because you've already missed part of the school day."

"I'm sure they would make an exception under the circumstances. Imagine the crowd that would come out for the game if I was there playing. There'd be people and reporters from all over the state."

"Yeah, I'm sure it would be crazy. And I'm sure you would thrive on the attention. But it's not going to happen tonight. Sorry about that."

She started crying.

He felt her pain, but there was nothing he could do to ease it. Or, at least, nothing he *was going to do* right now.

In Chemult, Oregon, Ken Roderick, Carly's ex-stepfather, was spending a lot of time thinking, and praying, about the situation with Carly. A remote part of him wanted to try to find her, try to rescue her. But after being completely shut out of her life for the past two years, on top of her mostly rejecting him for the five years prior to that, he had so far decided to let the law handle it.

He knew there was little he could do anyway. He was also smart enough to know the FBI probably had him under surveillance. So if he ever did figure out where she was, and managed to get close to her, he would be arrested again, no questions asked. No, this wasn't his problem, she wasn't his daughter anymore. And really, she *never was*, thanks to Grandma Windbag and her cult family followers.

The four law-enforcement agencies—the FBI, Oregon State Police, Roseburg Police and the Douglas County Sheriff's Departments—continued to follow each and every hint of a lead. So far, between the agencies, they had met and talked with the owners of over two hundred brown, mid-1980s, half-ton, two-wheel-drive Ford pickups, throughout Oregon, but had come away empty. Even the few that were spotted in the Umpqua National Forest were cleared.

Of course, no one in law enforcement even knew whether the pickup described by Bennie Vinn—the hippie who witnessed it coming out of Cherry Lane—was actually involved in Carly Cantwell's abduction. All the hours spent chasing down the owners of similar pickups may have been for nothing. But it was the only real lead they had to go on.

They also knew Cantwell could have been taken completely out of Oregon to who knows where. From the law's standpoint, each day that passed without finding her added a couple more nails to her coffin.

27

Brothers

Back at the falls, late-morning, Tuesday—

"Would you please take your mask off for me, Warden? I'm never going to identify you to the police. You've taught me a lot about myself that I needed to learn," Carly said, patronizing him, resorting to her well-honed manipulative tactics.

"So you admit that this time here is doing you some good," he answered, knowing full well what she was up to. "That's good. I knew you would eventually come around."

"Does that mean, you *will* take your mask off for me?"

"Not yet, but maybe soon," he said. "Now I'm going to tell you something that will shock you. But I think you're finally ready to hear it."

Instead of answering, she waited silently for his next great revelation, while she watched birds play at the edge of the water on the opposite side of the pool.

He let the breezy air around them grow pregnant for nearly a minute.

Then finally, "I'm your ex-stepfather's oldest brother."

"What? You can't be. His oldest brother is in an insane asylum. He's been there for years." Then putting two and two together, she stuttered, "You...you're...insane. That's why you took me, isn't it? That's why your voice sounds so familiar. You *are* his brother. How did you get out?"

"Is that what he told you all these years, that I was in an asylum?"

"But if you were in an asylum, how did you see him? You said you talked with him, but that you just hadn't seen him in quite a while. I'm confused."

Now she understood why he kidnapped her, and talked about the stuff he did. He was crazy. When you're crazy nothing has to make sense to make sense. And most crazy people were capable of murder and worse... God help me, please, she prayed silently. You can't reason with an insane person. They play along with you, but in the end, in their minds, they can justify whatever horrible thing they do to you. I can't believe a word he has said.

Maybe he hadn't talked to Ken at all. Or maybe he did in his mind, but not for real. But if he didn't talk with him, how did he know some of the things he knew? Yes. Crazy people find things like that out through their supernatural channels. Through their contact with demons and Satan.

Maybe he wasn't actually at my basketball games either. He couldn't have been. They would have recognized him and hauled him away in their white jackets.

Maybe the daughters he told me about weren't really his daughters. Maybe he just made them his daughters in his mind so he would have an excuse to kidnap all the other girls, the girls whose dried blood is on the floor... the girls he took away from everything they ever knew to hold hostage, to teach them his stupid lessons... just like me... b*efore he killed them.*

"Carly?"

"Carly?" he said louder.

She startled, "Wha... What?"

"My brother told you that I was in an asylum?"

"Yes."

"Did he say which one?"

"No. He only mentioned it a couple times, and that was in answer to one of my questions about his family."

"What if I told you I wasn't in an asylum? That I'm not crazy."

"I would believe you," she lied. Who would ever admit to being in an asylum? Everyone would think you were still crazy. And you would be. Crazy people never get better.

Then she remembered the fir trees he found. It didn't take much to set crazy people off. Oh God, please don't let him go off the deep end. Please don't let him go on a killing spree because of those trees. Why did you let Jeff and the others leave them where he could find them? Don't you care about me, God?

"Well that's good," he said. "That's very good. Then we can continue working on you."

"Working on *me*?" she stammered.

"Yes. Covering the kind of ground we've covered so far."

"You mean talking about Ken."

"Talking about your step dad."

"Right. My step dad."

"I know finding out that I'm actually your step dad's older brother is quite a shock for you. So right now I'm going to leave you alone for the rest of the afternoon. You need time to relax and regroup. Later, I'll explain why my brother told you what he did about me being in an asylum."

She didn't answer. She knew the routine by now. She went inside, so he could pull the ladder down. She knew better than to try to sneak a peek. Especially now. Now that she *knew* he was crazy.

Fifteen minutes after he left, she went outside and went right to work on the rope. She had to get the rope finished and get away before he moved her, or did to her what he did to the other girls.

At five o' clock she quit. She figured the moss-rope was only a couple feet shy of forty feet long now. That was enough. Tomorrow, after he left in the morning, she would escape. She put the rope in her hiding spot, got a long, cool drink from the creek and went inside.

Ten minutes later, he opened the door.

She sighed. Then she saw it.

Coiled at his side, in his right hand.

Her moss-rope.

She turned white as a ghost. He would kill her now.

He closed the door and stood in the light of the oil lamp on the table to his left. The right side of his mask was shaded, making him look terrifying now that he had the rope.

"What were you planning to do with this?" he asked.

She couldn't speak. Her mouth was dry, her throat frozen.

He tossed her coiled rope onto the floor between them.

She drifted back to a time in second grade. She was in the school librarian's office... sitting... waiting... The librarian walked in, looking stern and flopped a book down on the table in front of Carly. "Why were you writing in this book?"

She'd been caught. She trembled. She couldn't speak. Her mouth was like a desert, her throat frozen in fear.

"You will pay for a new book for writing in this one," the librarian said.

"I'll pay for it," Carly suddenly said aloud.

"You'll pay for what?" Warden asked.

"For writing in the book."

His heart broke. Who was the crazy one here? Was he driving *her* insane?

"What book? Did you write in one of my books?"

"What?" she said, her mind back to the present.

"What book were you talking about? You said you would pay for writing in the book."

"A book in second grade. I wrote in a library book in second grade. I had to pay to replace the book."

"Oh, I see. And my question about the rope took you back to the book in second grade?"

"I guess."

"Well, what were you planning to do with this rope you've made?"

"You already know the answer to that. Why do you continue to torture me? You know exactly what I was going to do with the rope."

He grabbed the end of the rope and pulled it up to examine it, while he sat down in the chair next to the table.

"This is very good work, Carly. I'm impressed."

"Stop!" she begged. "Stop playing your mind games with me. Just get it over with. Do what you're going to do. I can't take it anymore." She broke down sobbing.

He wanted to hold her, to make her pain go away; to make her fear go away. But he knew he would only make things worse if he touched her now.

"I think it's best that I leave you alone for now, Carly. But I'm going to keep the rope—at least for now. I'm glad you found a project like this to keep you busy. I knew you would."

She continued crying.

He left.

All her hard work... useless.

Her escape plan... foiled.

Completely at his mercy now... the crazy brother.

And I admitted to him that I rejected his brother. He probably brought me here to make me pay for what I did to his brother. That's why he's torturing me mentally. Next, he'll torture me physically. Then he'll kill me... for rejecting his brother.

But why would he care if I rejected his brother. His brother clearly rejected him all these years. To say he's been in an asylum. Insane. That's got to be the worst kind of rejection.

She fell asleep, mentally and emotionally exhausted. She awoke during the night, hungry. She used the bathroom, then ate some French bread and a banana. She climbed back into the sleeping bag. She lay there thinking.

Then Happy came.

"Oh, Happy. It's worse than I thought" she said, as she stroked his back. "Warden's crazy. He found my rope. I'm never getting out of here alive. What can I do?"

But Happy was oblivious to her predicament, as he rubbed up against her, eating up her affection.

28

Mental Ward

Wednesday morning, in the shack, 8 days missing—
After breakfast,
"Carly, do you want to know how your team did last night?"
"Of course."
"You'll be happy to know—"
"They won. Of course, they won. South Eugene isn't squat. They never should have beat us the first time."
"Actually, they lost," he said.
"No way. There's no way we could lose to South Eugene again."
"Well they did. And it wasn't pretty."
"How did you find out? What was the score?"
"Like I've told you before, it doesn't matter how I found out. The score was 47 to 33.
"We only scored 33 points against South Eugene? That can't be."
"Oh it can be. It was. I thought you'd be glad to hear that, to learn that your team lost a game because you weren't there."

"Of course I'm not glad about it. Yes, I want my team to miss me. Who wouldn't? But I don't want them to lose, especially when it can affect our standings and our rating in the state polls."

"Ratings are over rated," he said. "They always have been. The only thing that matters is what happens on the floor, between the baselines, for those thirty-two minutes."

"You've got to let me go home. You can't make my team pay any longer for whatever it is you're trying to make me pay for."

"You all-stars never have been able to see the good it does your teams when you can't play, whether your absence is because of being sick, injured, or something like this."

"Like any other all-stars have ever been taken, like this. How can it possibly be good for a team when its best players don't get to play? They lose games because of it."

"You see, Carly, you're so wrapped up in your own self import-ance that you can't see the bigger picture. The season isn't about one game, or even a few games. It's about the entire season: prepar-ing for the playoffs and the state tournament. Sure it's nice to see that occasional great team go undefeated and win the state championship. Everyone loves a story like that. But life isn't about state champions. There can only be one state champion. Life is about all the teams, about how they do the best they can. How their players build individual and team character by learning to truly function as a team, by overcoming adversity. It's not about one player, or even half a dozen players. It's about *the team*. You being gone is the best thing that could happen to your team right now."

"Thanks for the pep talk. But who died and made you the expert on high school athletics and what's best for my team?"

"There's a lot that you don't know about me, Carly. Kids are funny that way. Their worlds revolve completely around them-selves. They see all those parents in the stands and they don't know anything about any of them. And they rarely care to know. Many of those parents sitting in the stands at your basketball games played on teams just like yours, and thought just like you girls do now—

that the whole world revolved around them and their sports, or whatever else they were involved in. But when they grew up and had families, most of them realized that sports, or boyfriends, or choir, being or not being homecoming queen, was just a small part of what life is really all about. Unfortunately some people try to relive their lives through their kids. They're often the parents who yell the loudest, and harp on the referees the most, when their kids are competing."

"When are you going to stop with all these lectures?" she objected.

"Are you even listening to me, Carly? Am I completely wasting my time? Or is that just how you as a teen have to respond? You have to act like you don't listen or care about anything adults try to teach you?"

"You're a crazy man—and I'm supposed to listen to you?"

"Carly, I'm not crazy. I was only in the mental hospital for eight months."

"You're lying. Why would Ken tell me that you were there all those years if you weren't?"

"Because *they thought I was there*."

"All those years and they thought you were still there, in the insane asylum. I don't believe it. How can that be? And why were you there at all?"

"Okay, Carly. I'm going to explain it to you."

"Okay."

"I'll start from the beginning, kind of."

"**When** I was in junior high and high school, our family lived in the country outside of The Dalles, Oregon, not far from the Columbia River. When I was a senior, your step dad, Ken, was just in eighth grade. As you know, we had another younger brother and a younger sister."

"Beginning early my junior year, I had a girlfriend, the same age as me. When we weren't out doing all the things that teenagers do, we spent a lot of time at either of our homes. Her family loved me, and mine loved her. By late the next summer we knew we wanted to get married after we graduated the following June. Then one day in late September, everything changed."

"You guys broke up?"

"I wish."

"What happened?"

"I took my girlfriend to a party where they were smoking marijuana and trying some other drugs, some harder stuff. I had only tried pot a few times before that. My girlfriend—"

"What was her name?" Carly interrupted.

"I can't tell you her name. I don't remember. It's the only way I could deal with things."

"Deal with what?"

"If you'll let me go on, I'll tell you. This isn't easy for me."

"Okay."

"Anyway, my girlfriend smoked a little pot and liked it. So I thought if she liked it that much, she would really like some of the harder stuff. I had tried LSD once, a couple weeks earlier, and had a pretty good trip, so I thought she'd like that."

"Don't tell me—"

"Please, Carly, don't interrupt me," he said, obviously irritated.

"She somehow got some bad stuff or something," Warden went on. "She started having seizures, and then lost consciousness. Since all of the rest of us were high, we all figured it would wear off after awhile, so no one called the police. Plus no one wanted to get busted for doing the drugs.

"Well, an hour after she took the LSD, she stopped breathing. This beautiful, vibrant girl that I was going to marry died right there, that night, because of me. I'm the one who handed her the LSD-laced sugar cube that killed her. I'm the one who encouraged her to eat it. Me, her boyfriend. I killed her."

Carly felt compassion for him.

"I was freaking out. Someone finally called the police. Most the kids left before the police got there, but not me. I knew I had killed her.

"When the police arrived, they immediately called an ambulance. But, of course, it was too late. When they asked what happened, I admitted I had given her the acid, or whatever it was. They arrested me on the spot and hauled me off to jail where I continued to freak out. They brought in a psychiatrist to give me some tranquilizers and to try to help me. But there was no helping me. I went off the deep end. The guilt and her death were more than I could take.

"After several days, they hauled me away to the state mental institution, and that's where I spent the next eight months."

"What did your family do? Did they come see you?"

"My mom and dad came to see me a few times the first couple months. I didn't know who they were. I was gone. In a different world. I couldn't deal with what I had done. When they saw how screwed up I was, and that I wasn't getting any better, they quit coming. I think they were ashamed of me. Ashamed that I had killed my fiancee. That I was crazy. And I'm sure they had to listen to all kinds of negative things people in the community said about me and the situation, maybe even about how they had failed as parents. Who knows? I can only speculate."

"Were you ever charged with a crime?"

"I can only tell you what I heard after I got better. That's how I learned about my parents' visits too, after I got better. I heard that initially the state was going to charge me with involuntary manslaughter, but ended up dropping the case because of my mental condition and because other kids at the party said that my girlfriend asked for the LSD and took it on her own."

"So what happened after you got better?"

"I guess at about the five month mark of my time in there, I made a dramatic turn-around. The nurse came in one day, and I was there, the real me, the old me—other than I was heavily sedated and miserable. But my mind was back. They didn't talk to me about the girl at all. Not at first. They wanted me to get completely stable, cut me back on the meds to see how I did. Eventually they explained what happened, worked me through it with group and individual therapy, cut off all my meds, and finally released me."

"Did you go home?"

"No. In fact, I told the staff of the hospital that I never wanted to see my family again. They had deserted me in my time of need. The staff was not to give my family any information about me from that point on. I was eighteen by then, so they were obligated to honor my request."

"You never saw your family again after that?"

"Well, no and yes. I actually took on a new identity after that. Changed my name, everything. But after a lot of years passed, I was curious about my family, actually my younger siblings. I eventually made contact with Ken and told him what I had done, that I changed my identity. I didn't tell him my new name, where I was living, or even give him a way to contact me. I just told him I would keep in touch from time to time, and to never reveal anything about me to anyone else, including my other family members. As far as they were concerned, I was still institutionalized."

"So that's why he told me you were in an asylum?"

"That's right."

"Then why did you act surprised when I told you he said that to me?"

"At that point, I didn't know I was going to tell you about all of it. Besides Ken, I've never told another soul, except you."

"Well, I'm glad you did," she said. "I just don't know how much of it, or anything else you've told me, that I can believe."

"I know," he said. "You think I'm still crazy, don't you?"

"Why wouldn't I? I'm here, aren't I?"

"It won't be too much longer, Carly. But I'm going for a walk right now. We've covered enough ground, for the time being."

"Will you take your mask off when you come back?"

"I don't know. I'll think about it."

29

Carly's Part

Wednesday afternoon, at the pool, outside the shack—

"Please, Warden, take off your mask," Carly said.

"Not yet. Right now I need to tell you some important things you didn't know about your step dad and moms' relationship."

"You don't give up, do you?"

"I have my reasons," he said. "Did you know that before your mom married your step dad, he had been praying for two years that he could meet a woman that had a young daughter?"

"He did?"

"That's right. He always wanted a daughter. Then when he met your mom, he knew he would get you for his daughter."

"That's why he loved me so much, why he played with me so much back then, isn't it?"

"That's right. He saw you as God's answer to his prayers."

"Well things sure went to hell in a hand basket after that."

"I'll tell you something else I doubt you know: something ironic and terribly sad."

145

"I'm listening."

"Before your mom met and married your step dad, she and your grandmother prayed that she would meet a Christian man who could be a good father to you."

"I forgot about that. Yes. I remember right after the honeymoon, Mom and grandma told me that. They said God had answered their prayers. I forgot all about that. I was so young. And things got so bad later."

"Do you believe God answered your mom's and Ken's prayers?"

"How could he have? The relationship went in the toilet, they're divorced. Obviously it wasn't God's will."

"So you believe that whenever anything—like your mom and Kens' marriage—goes wrong, that is proof that God wasn't involved in it at all?" he asked.

"He couldn't have been, or it would have worked."

"Don't you think God sometimes starts a process, but then lets it play out naturally? Or that much of the time he doesn't involve himself in what goes on at all? He just sits back and watches?"

"What kind of a god starts something good and then lets it go bad?" she said. "Or what kind of god can let all the bad go on in the world and not do something about it? What kind of a god let's a man like you take a girl like me? All of that tells me that he doesn't care. Or maybe that he doesn't even exist."

"Do parents make everything turn out perfect for their kids, Carly? Do they control everything and everyone around them so their lives are perfect with no difficult times? Do they protect them from everything that is within the parents' control?"

"Of course not," she said. "That wouldn't be much fun for the kids if their parents controlled everything and did everything for them."

"So why do people think God should fix everything for them, make everything right?"

"I don't know," she admitted.

"I don't either," he said. "But what I do know is that God did fix the biggest problem that every person has: the problem of their sins separating them from Him and landing them in hell after they die. By sending His son Jesus to Earth to live and die for all mankind, he gave each person the opportunity to spend eternity with Him in heaven rather than in hell where they deserved to go—

"Enough of the sermon; I've heard that message all my life in church. I don't need to hear it again from you of all people. How hypocritical can you be anyway?" she said, shaking her head.

"You wanted to blame God for causing bad things to happen or for not fixing everything. No matter how it may look sometimes, *God is good*. It's people that do bad things, not God. So don't blame Him. As a matter of fact, people are often the cause of the bad things that happen in their own lives, and can cause bad things to happen in other people's lives. What if I told you that your grandma was the biggest reason that your parents' marriage failed and you were also a big reason?"

"I could believe Grandma had a big part in it. In fact I do. But everyone knows kids can't cause a marriage to breakup."

"So you don't think that all the times and ways you rejected Ken didn't contribute to the marriage problems?"

"What are you getting at?"

"What if I told you that even with the big problems that your mom and step dad had—many of which were caused by your mom's inability to stop your grandma, your Aunt Maggie and your brothers from interfering in the marriage and household—that your step dad *still wanted* the relationship to make it. At least up until the last several months? Do you know even after things got bad between them, Ken would often lie in bed next to your mom who was facing away from him and put his arm over her while she slept, but then pull it back?"

"What? How do you know that? Why did he pull his arm back?" she said, as a tear trickled down each cheek.

"Do you really want to know?"

"Yes."

"Ken wanted to love her so much, and you."

"I don't get it."

"He wanted to love both of you so much and have the marriage be right and be your dad. But every time he put his arm over your mom like that at night, wanting everything to be right, he would remember how you treated him, how you rejected him, how you wouldn't let him be your dad, how all the relatives had taken all that away from both of you, how your mom had let it happen, had let you reject him. When he remembered that, he immediately pulled his arm back off your mom, rolled over facing away from her, and cried silently."

Carly couldn't speak. Tears flowed off her cheeks and fell onto her legs and the rocks beneath her.

"Ken said to me, 'As hard as all the interference from my in-laws was, I could have withstood that. But what crushed me was Carly's rejection. That was the one thing I just couldn't take on top of the rest of it. I resented Glenda for all of it, but I resented her most because her daughter rejected me and disrespected me. Her daughter's rejection, the fact that she was allowed to reject me and disrespect me from a young age, killed any feelings of romance I had for Glenda.'"

"But you can't *make* a kid like someone."

"But *you can* require them to show appropriate respect to that person, or pay the consequences. And you said yourself that originally you loved Ken. When your mom saw the damage that was being done to yours and his relationship by her family, she still could have made you show him proper respect, required you to address him properly, or withdrew privileges from you. Ken even suggested it. But she wasn't about to keep you from your sports or staying overnight at your friends, just because you were a "little" disrespectful to your stepdad."

"But I was just a kid. I still am. You can't blame me at all for any of it," she objected.

"*That is* the politically correct answer, Carly. At least you have that down."

"If my mom didn't make me respect Ken, why are you blaming me?"

"You already admitted earlier, that you enjoyed the power you had over him—the power to hurt him. You made the choice to reject him. You're a very smart girl, Carly. You know I'm right. You know that you hurt him deeply. Deliberately. You *know* you played a huge part in why their relationship failed, especially as you got older.

"Own up to your responsibility. For crying out loud, you can be the all-star point guard on one of the best teams in the state because you are so good and you know what you are doing. Own up to the fact that you knew exactly what you were doing when you constantly rejected your step dad. You were being a selfish little brat. And yet you weren't smart enough to figure out that you cheated yourself out of having the thing you really wanted most— the love of a dad. The chance to have your mom and dad in love with each other. *You did that.* Who's going to give you away when you get married some day? You don't have a dad to do it."

"Stop it," she cried. "Yes, I did do that. I helped ruin the marriage. I knew I was doing that when I did it. I don't know why I did it. I just couldn't help myself. I cheated myself out of having a dad. And I cheated him out of having me for his daughter. *I'm sorry, God. I'm so sorry for what I did.*"

Warden watched her brokenness and knew that he was finished. He had accomplished what he had set out to do. He had forced Carly to look hard at who she was, how she treated other people, how she had played a big part in the breakup of her mom's marriage.

30

Unmasked

Thursday morning, by the pool, 9 days missing—

Under the beautiful, clear, sunny sky, birds flitted around the edge of the falls, and splashed water on themselves at the edge of the crystal-clear, cold pool outside the shack. Warden sat on his favorite boulder, the boulder that had served as his counseling chair for so many hours. Carly sat nearby on the boulder that had been soaked with so many of her tears.

"So now you're finally going to take your mask off for me, right?" she asked him.

"You've been through a lot up here, so far, Carly. You have faced who you are. And I hope you take what you have learned and apply it to your life when you get back home."

"Are you taking me home now, that is, after you take your mask off?"

"No. I can't take you home. And I'm not sure I should take my mask off either."

"I already told you that I will never identify you to the police, if you do," she assured him.

"Okay, Carly, I'll take my mask off. But you'll wish I hadn't."

"Why?"

"You just will. Are you sure you want me to take it off?"

"Yes. Please, just take it off."

Warden reached up to the bottom of the mask with each of his gloved hands and slipped his thumbs under the edge by the neck.

She couldn't believe, after all this time, she was actually going to get to see him.

He gently lifted the mask off in one smooth motion and let it fall into the water.

Carly screamed,

A monster. He's a monster.

She turned away, screaming, horrified at what this creature was.

She slouched down behind her boulder, screaming.

She dared another look.

She saw tears flowing down the monster's face.

As she watched, the monster took its gloves, jacket and shirt off.

Deep red skin was mixed with small patches of white skin twisted in any which way all up and down the monster's arms and torso. The monster's face had no nose, but there were two large holes where a nose should be. There were no ears, no eyelids, no eyebrows, and no facial hair. The only hair was a disarrayed section that covered the left back half of its head. The monster's head resembled the shape of a man's, but the skin was not that of a man. The monster looked almost devilish, deep red and badly scarred.

She could hardly stand to look at it, but at the same time she couldn't take her eyes away. Is this the devil himself? But it has no horns on its head. Maybe it's a demon. Do demons have horns? Does Satan himself really have horns? If not, this could be him.

Neither the monster or Carly spoke. They just stared at each other, tears still streaming down the monster's face.

Finally, it said, "I'm sorry, Carly. This is why I didn't want to show you all this time."

She was relieved to hear the familiar voice that she'd been conversing with for all these days. But the voice didn't fit this monster. She didn't speak. She couldn't. Was any of this actually real? Maybe I'm just in the middle of a horrifically long nightmare. That has to be it.

She pinched herself as hard as she could on her right thigh to wake herself up. But it did no good. She was already awake.

The monster—Warden—whatever... whoever... reached down and grabbed its (his) purple Astoria Fishermen Booster Club jacket and then pulled out a newspaper clipping. He handed it to Carly.

She looked at the date and read it and the article title aloud,

September 17, 1998-
Man Still Missing After Astoria-Megler Bridge Accident"

"You can't be," she said. "You can't be the missing man. *Are you* the missing man?"

"Read the first paragraph, Carly."

She looked at the photos with the article and looked at the monster. She looked at the photo of the man again, and then looked at the monster again.

She read the first paragraph of the article—

Police reported that long-time Astoria resident Edward Don Bradley was still missing, and his body has not been recovered, following the fiery two-car crash early Saturday morning, September 15th, which killed sixteen-year-old Susan Hope Fitzgerald and seriously injured seventeen-year-old Bryan Allen Russell. According to Russell, the man believed to be Edward Bradley jumped from the 200-foot-high Astoria-Megler Bridge while his clothes were on fire. U.S. Coast Guard vessels are continuing to search the Columbia River estuary and the Pacific

Ocean for Bradley, but said the search would be called off in a day or so.

"*Are you* the missing man? The burning man who jumped off the bridge?"

"Yes, Carly," the monster answered. "*I am* the missing man. I am **Edward Don Bradley.**"

"But you said your name is Warden."

"That's right. Warden came from Ed*ward.* If I *had* told you who I actually was before now, things would never have happened the way they did. We never would have accomplished all that we needed to."

"So you really aren't my step dad's crazy brother? You can't be then, can you?"

"Yes, I am also your step dad's crazy brother. But I'm not crazy. I'm just burned, as you can see."

"I don't understand," she said. "None of this is adding up for me. You're still alive. Where have you been all this time? And how do you fit into Susan Fitzgerald's life, or the other girl? That part of your story wasn't true then, right? It couldn't be. You couldn't have been in the other truck the night she was killed if she was actually your daughter."

"Carly, everything I've told you has been the truth, even the part about my daughters. I *was* in the truck her boyfriend collided with. And I wasn't drunk, no matter what you ever hear. I hadn't even had a drink."

"How could that many bad things happen to one person?" she asked.

"I don't know. All I know is I hope you take this whole experience and let it change the way you look at yourself, your life, other people, what's really important. Life isn't all about Carly Cantwell. It's about each person. Each person matters. Even all those kids that you made fun of or thought less of. Even your step dad. The way you look at other people and the way you treat them is your chance to make a positive difference in their lives."

"What about my mom and grandma, and the others that can be so hateful and mean?"

"The truth is: God cares about each person. But there are some people who choose to ignore him, and there are some who choose to treat others contrary to his way even when they are, or claim to be, his children. And *many of them* will never see that they do that. Or even if they do see it, they will never change. All you can do for them is pray."

"What about Ken, my step dad? He's not my step dad anymore. What do I do about him? Am I supposed to try to make things right with him?"

"I can't answer that for you, Carly," Warden said. "You'll have to ask God. Then do what you believe you need to. But I will forewarn you, that some of the people you've hurt, including your step dad, may not be open to patching things up. Some people's pain runs so deep from the things that went on that they can't open themselves back up and take another chance of being hurt some more. And some things will just take time."

"If you've been alive all this time, how did you survive? There's so much I'm curious about. I mean, when you were burning and you jumped off the bridge, what happened when you landed in the water so far below? Did you swim to shore? With such horrible burns, you would have died if you didn't get medical help immediately. What happened?"

"I understand your curiosity, Carly. You've asked so many questions since we've been together. I've answered some of them and not answered others. At this point I can't answer anymore of your questions about me—"

"Why not?" she interrupted. "Why can't you tell me more about you? And why did you take *me*? Why was it you?"

"I'm sorry, Carly. There are some things that we will never know the answers to on this side of heaven. I can't tell you any more. Just know that there *was* a reason that it was *me* that took you. And there was a reason it was *you* that was taken. Now go from here and make a difference. I've been blessed to have been able to spend time with you. I have to go for a bit now. So you need to go inside."

"But—"

"No, Carly. That's all."

She got up and reluctantly walked toward the moss-covered cavern. She looked back every few steps, still not believing any of what she had just experienced.

After she was inside, Warden—Edward "Eddie" Don Bradley— climbed the cable ladder to the top of the bluff and disappeared into the forest.

31

Alone Again Unnaturally

Carly awakened from her sleep and lit the oil lamp on the table. She looked at her watch. It was 8:30 Friday morning. This was her tenth day away from home. Where was Warden? Where was Happy? She hadn't seen or heard either during the night.

She was hungry. She got up and ate a third of the loaf of French bread that was on the table and drank the water.

She went outside. It was another beautiful mid-February day. Her team was playing South Medford away tonight. Surely Warden would return soon. Surely he would help her to go home now. Maybe her coach would let her play tonight, if she could get home in time to catch the players' bus. She knew her conditioning wouldn't be the best now, not after ten days of sitting around doing nothing.

She washed herself off with a washcloth and hand soap at the pool.

She waited… and waited.

By noon, she began to get concerned. Maybe Warden had finally been caught. If he was, help should arrive soon. She expected to hear airplanes, or helicopters. People yelling her name.

But there was nothing.

Nightfall came and still Warden did not show.

She knew she couldn't wait for him any longer. She would find a way to escape tomorrow morning. She looked all around for her moss-rope thinking maybe he hid it nearby, where she could find it. But it was nowhere.

She went inside and ate the rest of the French bread. She lay on her cot and read some more. She wanted Happy to show up. She wondered where he had gone. She felt so all alone again. She finally drifted off to sleep.

Carly awoke Saturday morning feeling a terrible sense of dread. She didn't remember dreaming during the night. She felt deeply depressed and hopeless. She knew she had to get up and figure out a way to escape. She didn't think she could bear another day and night here—especially without either Happy or Warden. Maybe Warden had left for good and took Happy with him. That must be it. He said he had accomplished all he had set out to do.

Or maybe something bad happened to him. She couldn't imagine that he would have left her there with no way to get away; no rope.

She went outside and saw it was an overcast, but balmy day. The sky was filled with white cumulous clouds. She couldn't tell if it was going to rain.

She walked around to the edge where she had her accident with the root breaking loose. She lay down on her belly on the bedrock and stretched her head, shoulders and chest out as far as she could over the edge of the cliff while keeping enough weight back to not fall over. She looked the situation below over the best she could from there. There has to be a way to get down these falls, she thought. She knew she couldn't possibly escape by going up. And she knew she could never take enough time to make another moss rope. Why did he have to find the other one?

As she lay there feeling desperate, she got an idea. Maybe she could ride the water down to the bedrock slope twenty feet below. She knew it was risky. Chances are she would hurt herself real bad when she landed. But maybe there would be enough force from the water being deflected to partially break her landing, before carrying her the remaining distance down the sloped bedrock into the pool below. *That was it.* It was her only option.

The water was very cold, she guessed in the mid forties. So she knew she would have to spend as little time in it as possible. She thought some more and finalized her plan. Why didn't she think of this earlier?

The rope. She had focused all her energy on making the moss rope. And it certainly was the much safer method. But this would work. It had to.

She quickly pulled herself to her feet, then went inside and gathered up everything she would take with her. As she looked at the sleeping bag and the cot, it suddenly dawned on her that she could rip the canvas cot into strips and make a rope. Without a knife she would have to use a sharp rock. It would take too long. He could come back by the time she got the cot cut up and the strips tied together into a rope.

The sleeping bag.

She grabbed the clothes she was wearing when she was kidnapped, along with a change of underclothes and outerwear from the dresser. Clothes she had already washed and dried twice. She laid her Roseburg jacket out flat on the plank floor and put everything she would take with her on it, then zipped it closed. She tied off the bottom with a strip of towel material.

She grabbed the sleeping bag and carried it and her jacket full of clothes along the east bank of the big pool to the east side of the downstream falls. She tossed her jacket over the edge to the bedrock shelf below to the side of the bedrock ramp she would be landing on when she rode over the falls.

She stripped down to her bra, jeans and tennis shoes. She needed all the protection she could get on her lower body, but she didn't want to get any more clothes wet than she had to. She tossed the long-sleeve shirt and hat down to the shelf with the jacket.

Now was the scary part. She prayed, "Dear God, I don't deserve your help. I know that. But please, right now, just help me to get over these falls and land safely below. Help me to escape... to get home. Amen."

She walked along the east side of the pool, carefully looking the situation over completely and thinking things through. She laid the sleeping bag out and zipped it closed, then wrapped it around her mid-section, so that it was doubled around her backside, and she grasped it firmly. It would cushion her landing. She quickly got in the frigid water fifteen feet above the falls and lay out on her back in the middle of the pool, with her head upstream.

Immediately, she began drifting toward the falls.

She hyperventilated.

"God forgive me for all the wrong things I've ever done. Please protect me now."

Five more feet.

"Help me," she screamed as she went over the edge. She was engulfed in water and in an instant, it seemed, her rear and back hit on the bedrock beneath her. She felt no pain. She was swept down the sloped bedrock into the pool below.

It worked. She did it.

She quickly swam to the right bank, while keeping a hold on the sleeping bag. She didn't dare lose it; she might need it again. She climbed up on the bank and immediately removed all her wet clothes. She wiped herself off with the towel from her jacket. She laughed. "Thank you, God," she said out loud. Step number one complete.

As soon as she was dry, she looked around. There was no way out on either side of the canyon above her. In the nude, she walked as far downstream as she could before reaching the bend in the creek and the next falls. These falls were even higher than the one she had just come over. But there was a deep pool directly under the falls that she knew she could reach by jumping from the right ledge. She went back and put her wet shoes and bra back on for the jump. She grabbed the sleeping bag and everything else, brought them to the edge of the falls and threw them down to the right bank. She counted to herself, one, two, three; she bent her knees and jumped out into the air. At the instant she hit the water below she tucked herself up tight into a ball, to keep from going too deep.

In no time she was up on the bank next to her belongings. She stripped and dried again, then looked things over at this new level.

Downstream forty yards was the next drop off. But just above the falls, she observed an old dead fir log about three feet in diameter lying across the canyon with its broken top resting on the bedrock on the left side of the creek, while its butt and roots were within a couple feet of the top of the cliff wall. The log lay at about a thirty-five degree angle, but it was loaded with thick moss.

Carly knew she could climb the mossy log to reach the top of the bluff and be on her way. She went back to her stuff and decided she wouldn't need the sleeping bag any longer. She took it to an old deadfall at the edge of the sheer cliff wall and crammed it behind the log. She didn't want Warden, or Edward, whatever his name was, to find it and figure out how she escaped.

She was suddenly overwhelmed with fear.

What if Warden is watching me right now? Maybe he's been here all the time, waiting, watching. Maybe this is just another one of his psychological ploys. Maybe he's going to wait until I reach the top, then come out of the bushes and say, "I'm impressed, Carly." Just like he did when he found the rope. God, don't let him still be here.

She quickly grabbed all her belongings, walked downstream to the narrowest part of the long pool, a spot about ten feet wide, and threw everything to the other bank. Her packed jacket landed inches from the water, and teetered there. She immediately dove into the pool and glided the short distance—her beautiful, naked body streamlined—and climbed up the opposite bank. She then grabbed her pack and moved away from the water.

After drying herself off and dressing in the clothes she was kidnapped in, she slipped on the low-top tennis shoes that she'd gotten from the shack. She wished she had used them during her jumps instead of her high top shoes. The high tops would have been better for hiking in.

When she had everything assembled and had gotten a long drink of water, she crawled up the old moss-covered log to the top of the east-bank bluff. She felt like yelling at the top of her lungs, "I'm free," but restrained herself.

Just then she heard and saw rustling in the Oregon grape bushes ahead of her. She screamed. It's him. But then she saw it.

A blue grouse.

She sighed. She forced herself to take long, deep breaths. It's okay, she told herself. You're okay.

She looked at her watch. It was only 10:08. She had all day to hike. The quicker and farther she could get away from these falls the less likely that Warden would catch her.

She took out one of the peanut butter and jelly sandwiches she had made and ate it. She felt confident she could get all the water she needed this time of year from seeps along the side of the mountain. Her step dad had taught her lots of different ways to get water from nature; the winter and spring months were the best. Water was abundant then.

She thought the road they had driven in and finally parked on couldn't be more than a mile and a half away to the east. She took off in that direction. After going a couple hundred yards, she thought she heard a helicopter. Then she was sure she did.

Are they looking for me? They must be. She looked around for the nearest opening where she could wave at the chopper. But it was nothing but trees around her for as far she could see. Should she go back to the creek canyon?

But the helicopter just made one pass high above the canopy of trees over her and was gone. It couldn't have been searching for her, she told herself.

She continued hiking.

32

The Road

After forty minutes she reached a gravel road. Is this the one we came in on?

She had no idea. It must be.

She decided to hike down the road, but she would have to keep her eyes and ears alert so she could hide in the woods if a vehicle came along. She had to be certain a vehicle wasn't Warden's before she showed herself. But she wasn't even sure what *his truck* looked like.

It had been too dark that night to be sure of the color. She thought it was either brown or a faded green color. The dash was brown. She knew it was an older truck, but she wasn't sure how old. She wished she knew more about trucks and had paid more attention when they were near the truck. But she had been too scared to think of anything but what he was going to do to her.

After she had walked for half an hour on the road, heading north, she came to a tight left-hand curve in the road. As she approached it, she was nervous that she could get caught here before she could hide. She contemplated getting far enough off the road on the corner to not be seen by Warden if he came by. But then she worried that if someone else came, she wouldn't be able to get into the open in time to wave them down.

She stayed on the road.

Just as she had come out of the curve, she heard an engine on the road behind her. She jumped over the right bank and ran for the brush just as the truck came into sight. Had she been seen? She heard the truck downshift just before it got even with her.

God no, it's him. He saw me.

The brown, 1985 Ford half-ton, two-wheel-drive pickup stopped on the left shoulder about twenty yards ahead of her.

She crouched as low as she could. Why did she have the black jacket on? She glanced around to see if she would blend in with her surroundings.

God, please blind his eyes. Don't let him find me.

She strained her eyes to read his license plate. She said the letters and numbers over and over in her mind to memorize them.

She expected him to get out of his truck any second. But then he revved the engine and continued slowly down the road to the northwest.

Is he messing with my head again? Does he even know I'm gone? God, I've had enough of this. Please. He had to have seen me, or he wouldn't have stopped. Where's he been anyway? He couldn't have been watching me in the woods or he would have stopped me before now.

Then she saw them.

A hundred yards away.

Four deer. A young blacktail buck deer and three does. They were headed to her right. That's it. They crossed the road in front of him, and he stopped to watch them, to let them go.

It was *just the deer*.

He hadn't seen her.

She was still safe. She broke down crying.

She walked back to the road and continued on to the northwest and then the road turned mostly west and rejoined a large creek. She figured it had to be the creek she had come from. She had no way of knowing if this road would take her out to a main highway, but she thought it might. She knew creeks always flow toward larger bodies of water, and there were always main roads near those.

She walked and walked—always alert for any vehicles that might come down the road, especially his. She got lucky once. It wouldn't happen again.

Then she heard it.

Someone was coming, from behind her.

She hurried into the brush on the right side of the road. She looked at her watch. It was 2:20 pm.

As the vehicle approached from the direction she had come from, she saw it was an older blue pickup with the back full of firewood. Could this still be him? Maybe this is another one of his tricks? She started shaking.

Then she saw there were two people in the vehicle. It couldn't be him. As the truck got closer, she was pretty sure the passenger was a woman with long hair.

She sprang out of the brush and climbed up the bank, waving her hands and shouting, "Help me; please, help me," over and over again. She was crying.

The truck came to a stop thirty yards from her. She thought she heard another vehicle coming from behind her, from the northwest. Oh God, don't let it be him.

But then there was nothing but the sound of the blue pickup's idling engine.

A woman, in her late fifties, got out of the right side of the truck and said, "It's okay, honey. What's wrong? What are you doing out here?"

Carly squatted down, bawling.

The man, also in his late fifties, got out from the left side, and said, "You're safe now. Everything's okay."

They both walked quickly up the road toward Carly. When they reached her, the woman knelt on one knee and put her arms around her. Carly's body heaved as she bawled. The man bent down and wrapped his arms around both of them, and kept saying, "It's okay. You're safe now."

After a minute, Carly settled down. They all stood up.

The man said, "What are you doing out here by yourself? What happened?"

Carly wiped the tears from her face with her hands, then said, "I'm Carly Cantwell. I was kidnapped eleven days ago from the Roseburg High School Parking lot. Where are we?"

The couple looked at each other, puzzled, and the man said,

"You were kidnapped from the high school?" They seemed clueless. Carly thought everyone in the state—and maybe in the nation—would know about her. "Can I use your cell phone?" she asked.

"We don't have a phone with us. We just live about twenty minutes farther down the road. This is Little River Road."

"You don't mean Little River Road off the North Umpqua Highway, do you?"

"Yes."

Carly broke into tears again. All this time she'd been less than forty-five miles from home, as the crow flies. The man and woman looked at each other and thought: this girl's really been through hell.

The woman said, "Honey, you said you were taken from Roseburg High School eleven days ago. We haven't heard anything about you because we live at our home in the woods and don't watch much television or listen to the radio much. I guess we missed the reports. But you're safe now. We'll take you to the sheriff's station."

At the Douglas County Sheriff's station, an hour and a half later, Carly was in a meeting room with her mom, brothers, sister, Jeff, and several law enforcement officers, including Bond Hampton.

They fed her some hot, cheesy lasagna, green salad, and a couple chocolate milkshakes, while her family huddled around her.

After Carly finished eating, Detective Bond Hampton began the interview with her by asking what the guy had done to her, if she'd been physically hurt, what type of living accommodations she'd had, and so forth. She answered the questions and told the officers about the newspaper clippings, and that it was Edward Don Bradley that took her.

She then described the details of her escape, including the scare she had when he had stopped near her in his pickup.

"Did you see his license plate?" asked Hampton. "Did you get his license plate number?"

"Yes. I got his plate number. I memorized it. It was 'CZM634.'"

"You're sure of that?"

"Absolutely. I remembered the letters by saying, 'CraZy Monster, CZM. And the numbers were easy for me to remember."

A deputy left the room, then came back several minutes later. He asked Carly, "Are you sure it was an Oregon plate?"

"Yes, I'm sure."

"Lieutenant Hampton, there are no plates in the Oregon DMV files by the number she gave us."

"Are you certain about the plate number, Carly?" Hampton asked.

"I have no doubts."

Everyone in the room, including her family and the law officers looked back and forth among themselves, many of them thinking, with the trauma she's been through chances are she's just mistaken.

"Okay, Deputy Marsh, get into the archived DMV files and see if that plate is in there. I know it's a shot in the dark, but maybe the guy hasn't renewed his plates in a long time. If he's been alive all this time and kept a very low profile, maybe he picked up an old truck years ago and never updated its registration."

A few minutes later Deputy Marsh returned and said, "I've got something. This plate number *was* registered to Edward Don Bradley, but the vehicle connected with it is the 1985 brown Ford pickup that was destroyed in the fiery crash on the Astoria-Megler Bridge on September 15th, 1998. Something isn't adding up."

"Something definitely isn't adding up," said Hampton, a quizzical look on his face.

He turned to Carly and said, "The license plate number you gave us is the same one from the vehicle that Bradley wrecked over eleven years ago. Is it possible that he told you the license plate number of that vehicle while he held you captive, and you've just gotten confused? You've been through a lot."

"No," she said, her eyes getting watery. "He never told me any plate numbers. I actually got a good look at the pickup's rear plate when he was stopped just down the road from me. I'm telling you the truth. CZM634 was the plate on *that* pickup. I'm a hundred percent sure."

"We've got hundreds of cops and FBI agents in and on the way to the Umpqua National Forest and along the North Umpqua Highway right now, Lieutenant," said the FBI commander. And we have two helicopters and two fixed-wing airplanes in the air. Even if, somehow, she has the license number wrong, we still have an excellent chance of catching that monster."

"I'm not wrong," Carly insisted.

"I believe you, Carly," the commander said. "I'm just saying that if we can catch the guy in that area, the plate number doesn't matter anyway."

"Will you be willing to go back into the Little River area with us, Carly?" asked Hampton. "Will you go with us and take us to the falls where you were held captive?"

"Yes, but I'm worn out right now," she answered.

"I understand that. How about if we give you your own time tonight and tomorrow, then we will go in first thing Monday morning. It's highly doubtful he's going to stay there anyway once he finds you've escaped. That is, if he even goes back there. Between the FBI, OSP and our Sheriff's Department, all the roads out of that area are secured. If he's still in there, he's not getting away."

"Yes," she said, your plan sounds good, officer. Besides I have a lot of catching up to do with my family and friends between now and then. Plus I need to get a lot of time in on the basketball court to start getting myself back in shape. My team needs me."

"They sure do," Hampton said. "Great to have you back, girl. You get some rest, now."

33

Conclusion

On the late local-news, Saturday evening—

Roseburg teenager Carly Cantwell was found safe and sound today on Little River Road in the Umpqua National Forest. Cantwell has been missing for eleven days, since her abduction from the Roseburg High School parking lot following her game Tuesday night, February 2nd.

FBI and local law enforcement officers have identified Cantwell's abductor as Edward Don Bradley. Bradley was previously believed to have died following the fiery roll-over crash he was involved in on the Astoria-Megler Bridge in September 1998 that killed a teenage girl and seriously injured a teenage boy. At the time of the crash which occurred shortly after midnight, Bradley was reported to have jumped from the 200-foot-high bridge while on fire. Since the U.S. Coast Guard never recovered his body, he was believed to have been swept out to sea on the strong outgoing tide. Bradley hasn't been seen or heard from since that accident over eleven years ago. When asked how they determined that the perpetrator was, in fact, Bradley—considering he was presumed dead all those years ago—Douglas County Sheriff Chad Wolvord said, "We are confident that Edward Bradley was definitely Cantwell's abductor. But there *are* a lot of unanswered questions surrounding him at this time. We are using all the manpower and resources available to bring him into custody."

When asked if local guard units would be utilized in addition to the hundreds of FBI, state and local law enforcement personnel, Sheriff Wolvord said, "At this time we have not asked for the army's assistance, but that remains a possibility. Obviously, we'll have a better chance of finding Bradley in daylight tomorrow. That's all I'm going to say at this time. Thank you. Oh, I would like to add, that if anyone sees or has information on the whereabouts of a brown, 1985, half-ton, two-wheel-drive Ford pickup, license plate number CZM634, please contact local or state law enforcement immediately."

An intense Douglas County-wide manhunt on the ground and in the air the next day, Sunday, February 14th, was fruitless in finding Edward Don Bradley.

Monday morning, February 15th, in the woods approaching the Little River Waterfalls—

"This is where I climbed up to the top of the canyon," said Carly Cantwell, over the noise of the stream below. "I crawled up that mossy log right there." She pointed below her, just over the edge of the bluff. "The cavern where he kept me is just upstream from here past the next two falls."

The dozens of law officers cautiously spread out and moved ahead along the east bank above the canyon, moving from tree to tree with their guns drawn.

The FBI commander yelled, "Bradley, this is the FBI. You are surrounded. Come out with your hands up and step over to the edge of the stream where we can see you."

No response.

He repeated his order over a megaphone several more times, but still nothing.

No surprise there.

Several of the lawmen then converged on the bluff overlooking the falls and pool where Carly had spent nearly eleven days. They looked all around the top of the bluff where Carly indicated the cable ladder should be stowed, based on where she had seen it from down below.

Nothing. No sign there had ever been a ladder.

Everyone, including Carly, was puzzled.

"It's got to be around here somewhere," she said. "It was attached to these two alder trees."

"There's no indication here that anything has been attached to these trees or that anything has hung over this bank."

"Well, I don't know what's going on here, but the shack is right down there behind all that stringy moss," she said, pointing below and to the left of the falls.

Detective Hampton immediately got on his radio and asked that a helicopter deliver a long cable ladder so they could get down to the shack.

Twenty-five minutes later, they had the ladder attached to the two alder trees—

Detective Hampton led the way down the ladder. They were all dying to see the shack. After several lawmen and then Carly were down on the shelf adjoining the long pool below the falls, Carly said, "It's right back in there. That's where he kept me. That's where I slept."

The lawmen brushed the spaghetti-like moss-strands aside and pointed their flashlights into the cavern, as Carly stayed close to them.

Immediately they spotted old, rough-sawn one by sixes hanging in disarray ahead of them. They suddenly felt better about what Carly had been saying. But when Carly saw the front of the shack, she said, "Something's wrong. Those boards were all nailed uniformly before. It's not the same. Maybe he came back and did that." They moved ahead several steps and opened the shabby door to the make-shift shack. As soon as Detective Hampton said, "Clear," Carly stepped in,

"The table and cot are gone," she said. "They were right there." She pointed to the left of the doorway and then to the back wall. She quickly turned to her right to show them the dresser that had held the books and the other girls' clothes. "The dresser was right there."

"He must have taken everything," said Hampton.

"But why?" said the FBI commander.

"You said there was a cat here, too, didn't you, Carly?" asked Hampton.

"Yes. It was a gray and white tom. He just called it 'the cat.' But I named him Happy." Then she suddenly thought of the blood spot she'd found on the floor.

"The blood spot on the floor was right down around in here." She pointed the beam of a flashlight around where the stain should have been. "I don't understand. It's gone. The blood stain is gone. He wouldn't have taken the time to wash that away, would he?"

"I don't know, Carly," said Hampton. "There's a lot about all of this that just doesn't quite add up."

The FBI agent was beginning to wonder if there wasn't a whole lot more to Carly's story than she had admitted to. And he wasn't the only one wondering. Hampton thought back to the morning following her disappearance, how he had asked Carly's mom if there was any chance Carly had arranged things to look like a kidnapping in an effort to gain more attention. She could have known this old miner's shack was up here all the time and knew it would make a great prop for her story.

Why would a kidnapper take her such a short distance from her home? Why didn't she answer when Jeff and the other students called her name? They were just downstream a short distance. It wasn't adding up.

Carly sensed the lawmen's silent skepticism, and said, "I'll show you the fire circle and where I hid my sleeping bag after I went over the falls, if you don't believe me."

"Don't say that, Carly," said Hampton. "No one's saying they don't believe you. It's just that things aren't quite the way you said they were. That would raise questions with anyone."

"Come on, Lieutenant Hampton; let me show you the other stuff."

She led the way around outside. She pointed out the fire circle, then where she had supposedly had the near fall on the root, where she had gathered moss from, and hidden the rope-in-progress, and then directed them to the deadfall where she hid the sleeping bag. Some officers got down there, but there was no bag.

She insisted on going back inside the shack one more time. Several lawmen followed her in. As she stood there in the room, obviously bewildered at the whole situation, she heard a familiar sound. She looked off to the right near where the dresser had been.

"Happy! It's you, Happy."

Happy crawled out the rest of the way from behind the loose board and walked over to Carly. She immediately squatted down and picked him up in her arms, and cried.

The officers didn't know what to think. Her emotions upon seeing the cat couldn't have been made up.

After a minute of tearful reunion with Happy, Carly stood up with him in her arms and said, "This is all so weird."

"You're not telling us anything." said Hampton.

"One time when Warden, or Edward, or whatever his name was, was talking to me about a book I had been reading, involving a couple kids and an angel, he asked me if I believed in angels. Then he went on to ask if I'd ever heard of the passage in the Bible that talks about being careful how we treat strangers because some people who thought they were just dealing with *strangers* were actually entertaining *ANGELS*. Is it possible? Could he have been...?" **

The officers looked at each other thinking she's definitely either made this whole thing up or gone off the deep end. But how could she have known that license plate number? And the cat?

One of the deputies said to Hampton and the FBI Commander, "*Is it possible...?*"

Carly looked back and forth from one face to another, wondering herself.

After thirty seconds, the FBI commander said, "Nah. It couldn't be. No way."

He led the way out of the shack. He and Carly (with Happy on her shoulders), and the rest of the lawmen, climbed up the cable ladder and hiked back out to the road where their vehicles were parked.

Late local and state-wide news, Tuesday night, February 16th—

Carly Cantwell led her Roseburg High School girls' basket-ball team to a convincing 63-41 win this evening over league rival Churchill. Cantwell received a standing ovation by everyone in the gymnasium when she was introduced before the game; then she went out and scored 17 points. Welcome back, Carly.

The three-day search for Edward Don Bradley by hundreds of local, state, and FBI law enforcement agents has turned up no sign of him or his 1985 Ford pickup truck. A spokesman for the agencies said the search will continue.

**Hebrews 13:2

An Interview with
Author Wesley Murphey

**Note- Do not read this interview before reading the book.

Lost Creek Book's Jill Curtis: Wesley, all of your other books to date have been directed toward the adult reading audience. Why did you write **Girl Too Popular** for teenagers?

Wesley Murphey: It's true that the Girl story is directed toward teenagers. But it is actually a story that many adults will enjoy as well. I've received great feedback from several adults who read the manuscript. I began writing this story because I've seen how problems between step kids and step parents are so common and how hard those problems can be on a marriage. I know that from my own childhood as well as from many other situations I've seen and heard about both as a kid and as an adult. I also know there are at least two sides to being one of the most popular kids in your school or neighborhood. So I thought, why not deal with both situations (most popular kid and stepkid-stepparent problems) in one story. Throw in my love for the woods and sports and run with it, which is what my mind did. I chose to have the abducted kid be a girl for several reasons—one of the biggest being that girls and women are by far the largest audience for fiction and this kind of story would be especially appealing to them because it gets to the heart. I know I didn't directly answer your question.

Jill: That's fine. The book's back cover asks whether Carly's abductor is connected to her ex-stepfather who she rejected or possibly to someone or something greater. It turns out both are true. The abductor *is* connected to the ex-stepfather *and is* also an angel. I thought it was clever how you introduced the angel idea into the story through a book Carly read while in captivity. Then she and her abductor asked each other if the other one believes in angels. Do you believe in angels, Wesley, or was that just a nice thing for your story?

Wesley: You bet I believe in angels, though I don't understand them very much. I know there are well over a hundred references to angels in the Bible.

Jill: I know this was a fiction story, but do you believe God would ever use an angel to actually kidnap someone? Why would God put someone through that kind of stressful, scary experience?

Wesley: I certainly don't understand the workings of God. But I do know the Bible says in many places that trials are good for us because they help build our character. I'm sure Carly's character will be positively affected by the trial she went through at the hands of the angel in this story. As far as whether an angel would, or has, ever kidnapped someone, I can't answer that one. I do know, however, that angels have caused stress for real people.

A great example of this is recorded in the Bible's book of Genesis where Jacob, one of Israel's spiritual fathers, wrestled with an angel in the form of a man one night and experienced pain and stress in that conflict. Yet he prevailed. In fact—because of Jacob's persistence during that trial as well as in previous trials—at the end of that conflict, God told Jacob (through the angel he had wrestled) that his name would no longer be Jacob, but was now *Isreal*. That's amazing when you consider that was the very moment when the nation of Israel actually received its name—4,000 years ago. Of course our savior, Jesus Christ, Emmanuel, also received his name from an angel, the angel Gabriel—2,000 years ago.

Jill: That *is* amazing. Have you ever encountered an angel?

Wes: Like many people, I believe I probably have, and I'm sure I must have had an angel's protection at one time or another, especially in some close calls when trapping rivers in the winter. But I can't say for sure. Who knows, maybe I entertained one without knowing it. The spiritual world is alive and well regardless of what people might say otherwise. God is as real as the oxygen we each breathe every minute of our lives, even though we can't see it or God. Of course we can clearly see God's attributes through His creation.

Jill: Your other new novel **To Kill a Mother in Law,** which was released at the same time as **Girl Too Popular**, has a connection to this book. Tell the readers about that.

Wesley: The main connection is that Carly Cantwell in this Girl book, is little *Jackie* in the mother in law book. The locations are completely different as are the circumstances; for example, Carly's grandma is still alive in this book. But readers will appreciate a closer look at the younger version of Carly. They will also recognize that Carly's ex-stepfather is the rejected stepfather who plays a huge role in the mother-in-law book. The mother book is much more graphic and deals with mature themes, so I can't recommend it for younger teens at all.

Jill: You have four non-fiction outdoor books coming out in 2013; do you have any other novels on the horizon?

Wesley: Actually I do have one; it's just a matter of when I have time to write it. It's about a deadly light in today's society that people are clueless about. I know when I do sit down to write I can really crank out the words. I wrote **A Homeless Man's Burden** (91,000 words) in thirty-eight days, though it required further editing. I wrote the **Girl Too Popular** manuscript in twenty-eight days.

Jill: That is really getting with it. Well, I hope you find the time to write it; you have my interest already.

About the Author

Wesley Murphey was born and raised in Dexter and Pleasant Hill, Oregon and lived in Lane County, Oregon until 2003, when he moved his family to beautiful Central Oregon. He and his beautiful wife enjoy going fishing, hunting, hiking, swimming, camping and doing numerous other outdoor activities together. With *Girl Too Popular* and *To Kill a Mother in Law* both released in 2012, Murphey now has six books in print, with four more scheduled to be released in 2013. Three of the four upcoming books will feature numerous outdoor articles written by Wesley and his now deceased father, Don Murphey. The fourth book will be a collection of many of Wesley's published articles on trapping.

See back of this page to order Wesley Murphey's books-

Lost Creek Books
PO Box 3084
La Pine, OR 97739
email: lostcreekbooks@netzero.com
website: lostcreekbooks.com

Wesley Murphey's books make great gifts!

Get more information and order more of Wesley Murphey's books at lostcreekbooks.com. Credit cards accepted. Or order through your local book store.

_____ Cut here _____

Quick order form for Wesley Murphey's books

Fiction:	Price	#books	Ext.Price
A Homeless Man's Burden	$14.95	____	_____
To Kill a Mother in Law	$14.95	____	_____
Trouble at Puma Creek	$14.95	____	_____
Girl Too Popular	$12.95	____	_____

NonFiction:

Blacktail Deer Hunting Adventures	$12.95	____	_____
Conibear Beaver Trapping inOpen Water	$11.00	____	_____
(Plus total shipping regardless of quantity)			$3.50

Total Price _____

Send check or money order to address at top of page. Be sure to include your name and address. A phone number should be included with large orders.